THE HILLS
OF APOLLO BAY

THE HILLS OF APOLLO BAY

Peter Cowan

Fremantle Arts Centre Press

First published 1989 by
FREMANTLE ARTS CENTRE PRESS
1 Finnerty Street (PO Box 891), Fremantle
Western Australia, 6160.

Copyright ©Peter Walkinshaw Cowan, 1989.

This book is copyright. Apart from any fair dealing
for the purpose of private study, research, criticism or
review, as permitted under the Copyright Act, no part
may be reproduced by any process without written
permission. Enquiries should be made to the
publisher.

Consultant editor B.R. Coffey.
Designed by Helen Idle and B.R. Coffey.

Typeset in 11/12pt Baskerville by City Typesetters,
Perth, Western Australia, and printed on 90gsm Print
Right by Lamb Printers, Perth, Western Australia.

National Library of Australia
Cataloguing-in-publication data

Cowan, Peter, 1914-.
   The Hills of Apollo Bay.

   ISBN 0 949206 44 X

   I. Title.

A823'.3

*For Edith
In Memory*

Acknowledgements

The cover illustration is reproduced from the cover of the journal *Angry Penguins* (No.8, 1945), by courtesy of the artist, Albert Tucker, and Max Harris. The epigraph by T.S. Eliot is from his *Collected Poems 1909-1962*, and is reprinted by permission of the publisher, Faber and Faber Ltd. The passage from Wright Morris, titled 'Martha Lee', reproduced on page 142 is from the journal *New Directions* (1940). Efforts to locate the copyright owner have been unsuccessful and the Publisher would appreciate any advice of current ownership. The untitled poem by D.B. Kerr on page 222 first appeared in the journal *Phoenix* (Adelaide University Union, 1939) and is reproduced courtesy of the Adelaide University Union.

The Hills Of Apollo Bay was published with the assistance of the Australia Council, the Australian Federal Government's arts funding and advisory body.

Fremantle Arts Centre Press receives financial assistance from the Western Australian Department for the Arts.

This is a work of fiction. Where actual people are referred to it is by name, as public figures in a time. No other reference is intended. A strict chronology of real events is not attempted.

Memory!
You have the key,
The little lamp spreads a ring on the stair.
    T.S. Eliot, *Rhapsody on a Windy Night*

It was very beautiful.
 The woman looked at her watch. She said: Beautiful? Where?
 The hills. At Apollo Bay. You remember.
 No, she said. I don't remember. I've never been there.
 The room quiet. Silence some part of the small clean space, the corridor beyond the open door, the other rooms, and the other corridors and the open wards, voices, people walking. She said: I think it's time I was leaving.
 Are you busy?
 I will be. I hope.
 I suppose it was romantic. Yes.
 Romantic?
 For us to go there. I think he despised it. Even then I thought that.
 Charles?
 It seemed a long way then.
 I doubt if my father despised a bit of romance. However far he had to go for it. The way he used to dress up. All those medals. Anzac Day. Occasions. Very handsome. But you are the romantic, mother. For all your hardheaded business success. It paid off in your business.

He never wrote about it.
I will come in tomorrow. I really do have to go.
Home.
Home, mother, is Sydney. I'm going with Richard.
She's coming to see the house, Jessica. He said: Kathy never has time.
You know I haven't had time.
He said: Of course.
Mother, I will come in tomorrow. I promise.
It was beautiful.
I'm sorry?
Her mother's face was still. Her head turned on the pillow. From the window the tops of the buildings, the trees and the small roofs of houses, the rise of land beyond the railway line, coloured streamers of the service stations, used car yards.
Tomorrow then. She bent towards her mother's face, touched her hand.

The wide windows framed grey scrub and the slope of dunes, the road and traffic. At one edge the angles of houses, broken, disordered, on the rising land. Framed carefully. A set. The moving cars. Perth changes, she said. Whenever I come back I see it.
Yes, he said. In its way.
It's strange my family ever came here. Very confirmed Victorians, actually. As you know. My dear father did get back there, of course. Rather sooner than we expected.
Beyond the road and the moving cars, the sea. The backdrop. Low clouds, and the light from the broken water.
Oh no.
I'm sorry?
That awful place. This reminded me. It's very impressive, Richard. And of course you will watch the America's cup from here.

If I knew what I was looking at. And had a powerful enough telescope.

I see. Will you voyage out there?

I will not. You were too busy to see this last time, as I recall.

Well I was.

It seemed sensible to sell the other place. We'd been there long enough.

And you came here. It's very prestigious.

I came here. Yes. I like this view. And being near the sea. Yes. And the girls like it here.

I'm sure. And Ann.

Places don't mean all that much to Ann.

Where is she?

She's gone with the girls to Singapore. The university vacation.

Of course. She lives here?

Ann has her own place. She stays here when she wants to. Kathy, you know all this.

Cosy. And she takes the girls away. How fortunate.

For them. Yes.

Lucky girls. It was harder for us, Richard. All this rushing about the world. Much harder for us.

At their age, I suppose it was. But it didn't restrict you. Later.

No, she said. She ran her hand slowly along the arm of the heavy lounge. And why aren't you with them?

Work. And, well, your mother.

I'm sorry. Richard, it is very good of you.

I'm fond of Jessica.

I know. You always did get on with one another. Better than I did. Or my long gone brother.

Let me get you another drink. I'm sorry the girls are not here.

She turned away from the glass. The glare from the water. The room comfortable. Neutral. For all the discreet furniture, expensive. All the houses with their careful views of the ocean perhaps the same. However desperate their facades. City Beach. A name without relevance. A line of drab names holding about all these beaches. Cottesloe. Scarborough. North Beach. A recital from her childhood.

How strange.

Strange?

The names of these beaches. I'd forgotten.

English, I suppose, some of them. Reminding someone of beaches at home. Once.

My god. How could they.

How could they. Kathy when you said that awful place. Which this reminded you of. What did you mean?

Not like that. No. I've been working in this terrible South Sea thing. Horrible really. An island. Which of course was not too far from Sydney. All surf and sun and bodies.

You are very brown. Sounds like your kind of thing, perhaps.

Maybe not any more. Tensions. Bad feeling. Terry just can't work with some people. You're not going to believe this, but they built this great native hut thing. Which was to burn with some effect. It had to be one off, of course. So in flames it went, everyone staggering from the burning wreckage. And the odd stunt men. The camera had jammed.

I suppose that can happen.

It depends. There was a lot of not speaking to one another for quite a time. Believe it or not I was a society matron. I did get to wear a grass skirt affair. Which I lost eventually. At the water's edge. Sunset. Like out there beyond your windows.

The famous boobs and bottom.

A little spread these days. Unfortunately.

I'm only jealous, Kathy.

You don't have to be.
Someone?
Not for a while. If you must know. Are you offering?
Not quite like this.
No, she said. Oh well. It's not any better, is it?
We could have dinner. Here. Or go out.
Yes. Here. We can fix something. I'd like that. She lifted her hands. That awful island. Promise you won't watch it.

She said: It is quite a splendid meal.
Mrs May leaves everything for us.
And the girls help.
I wouldn't say the kitchen was their favourite place.
No.
He said: I saw you a while ago. At one of those award nights.
You didn't watch that?
There you were.
There I was. Not receiving any recognition for my efforts actually.
I missed that part.
It had all been nicely arranged. Not too much bitching.
She was looking at him. Without expression. Mocking him. Or herself. He said: When I see you like that, among all those people, it's someone I don't know.
Not me.
I don't know.
But you are afraid it might be.
Do you think so?
Yes, she said. And I don't know if it is me. Sometimes I'm afraid it is.
They can't be real. Those people.
They have their masks.
I suspect they are their masks.
So do I, Richard.
I'm sorry, he said. I didn't mean to get round to

anything like this. Did you enjoy the evening?
　Yes, she said. I suppose I did.

The room in darkness without shape. The windows curtained, a faint light, nothing for her eyes, the walls endless. She said: Richard. Please.
　What is it?
　I don't even know where you are.
　Quite close.
　The light from the bedside lamp drawing shapes still distant. Softened. Age, she said. Tearing at my bones. Just hold me.

The curtains held a pattern of colour, greyed, obscure. The sheets of the bed neat, her fingers touched them. He came quietly into the room. A movement of the half-light. He said: I didn't wake you. But if you would like breakfast.
　I was lost last night, she said. But yes. And thank you.
　He drew the heavy curtains slightly. Without sound.
　That, she said, looks down to the sea, I suppose.
　Yes.
　It would have to. But it's too early to know that kind of thing.
　I jog down there. Along the beach on a good morning.
　Not this morning.
　Yes. A high tide. The beach was hard. Clean, except for the plastic rubbish.
　Is that bad?
　Always now. I'll get your breakfast. No changes?
　No.
　She drank the coffee, the small pieces of toast broken, pushed about the plate. A morning battle in which her fingers twisted nervously at some adversary he had never understood. He said: You are welcome to stay.
　I think I would like to.
　Then stay.

And I know I should. But I can't.

There are no problems, Kathy.

Oh yes. One, I have to go back today. There is this part in a series. Soap, yes. It may be quite horrible. But Richard there are just no good parts for someone my age. Few enough parts. Period. But at least I haven't got to making a fool of myself in daft tv ads.

Kathy you know you never need do that.

You don't understand. I don't think you ever did.

I do. And I don't.

If I miss this it will go to dear Alison. That I can't afford.

I'm sorry. If it is that way.

She moved the things together on the tray. Crushed the paper napkin. And there's us. We are not enemies.

No. I don't think we were ever that.

Even good for one another. In small doses. Lethal if taken to excess.

Well, as I said, I'm sorry.

It's for me to be that. And I am. And I shouldn't be leaving my mother. But I sit there and if she says anything I don't understand it. Part of the time she doesn't know I'm there at all.

I think she does.

It could just go on like that. I can't stand it.

The light beyond the window had hardened. In the room, filtered, but clear. She reached out her arms slowly, as if her fingers might test the light, her skin brown, firm, upper arms full, the curve to her shoulder.

She won't know if I'm not there. It's very strange. She has always somehow seemed to be able to slip away somewhere. I don't know. Just not there. I think as a child it frightened me. I used to try to make her see me. Oh god Richard all this is very early morning. I hate mornings. But it sent my father away. Oh, other things. But that, yes. And it made my brother a stranger. He went too. Canada. You can't go further than that. And now it's like this. Oh

shit. Richard. Please. As a favour.
He said: I wouldn't put it like that.

She held the thin robe about her and he opened the door. The smooth cement sweep of driveway with the clean garden beds. A long rectangle of lawn. He said: Take the other car. You can leave it at the airport. I'll have it picked up.
I can get a taxi.
No. I'll come out if I can.
I'll call at the hospital.
I think she would like that.
I haven't told her I'm going. I don't think she would remember, anyhow. It would do no good.
The car slid neatly down the drive. Into the traffic already along the road. Indistinguishable. From the upper window she looked down at the garden. Like an architect's drawing. All there. Everything that should be. And beyond it the dunes and the sea. Cold, clear in the early light.

Her mother seemed asleep. A television set placed across the bed, blank, silent, and she knew her mother was watching her.
You have the television, she said. There are some good things on that.
Her mother's hand moved. I don't think I understand it any more.
Who does. But it's been bread for a few of us.
Her mother watched the clear window space. Each morning the nurse drawing the curtains, the day there.
Richard sent his love, she said. And the girls. He'll be in to see you.
The girls are at school.
University, mother. They have gone on holiday.
It was too late.

Too late?
That I met your father. It was not my fault.
Of course not.
I think he did go to England. After the war.
I thought he came over here.
He had to wait.
Wait?
A passport. Papers. Though he never said anything. It was a long time ago, Kathy. He didn't think I knew. He would never say anything.

I don't know why my father would ever have had any trouble getting a passport. Are you sure?

I wanted to see if he would write about it. Whatever it was. He never did. But I wanted something out of it all. I was glad.

Yes, she said. There were flowers on the small shelf by the basin. Carnations, some deep red flowers, fronds of fern. The light from the window held the tops of the houses in clear colour. The glitter of the car yard streamers. Green. Gold. The deep green lawn where her mother always had the sprinklers going. You are wasting water, she said. No. The plants like it. And it makes the place cool. I'm going to get reticulation and a bore put down. The man is coming next month. My god, she said, you'll wash the place away. The deep beds of zinneas, petunias, gerberas. Lush fleshy leaved annuals, the leaves splashed purple, red. She had brought the fallen leaves in and placed them by her bed. Carefully, on the small dressing table. Her mother never removing them, and they dried slowly. Heavy shrubs her mother argued about with the gardener. They need only light pruning. You take too much from them. People passing in the street to look at the garden. She had not been back there. Her mother seeing the garden grow beyond her. To leave, and the expensive, fashionable home unit. Pot plants in strange profusion on the cement balcony. They will fall off one

day, mother, and kill someone down there.
 They never did, did they.
 No, she said. And for a moment in the small white room was startled. I'll have to go soon. Is there anything I can get you?
 Come tomorrow.
 If I can.
 I've been trying to remember. I meant to tell you.
 Tell me now.
 I can't remember exactly.

Almost at the last minute, before the flight call. A script timing. As perhaps it was. She turning to face him.
 I'm glad you came.
 I thought the traffic had beaten me.
 You hardly have traffic here, she said. Richard, when you see my mother, ask her if she wanted to tell me something. She was just being stubborn this morning, I think. My god, she could always be that. But if it is anything, could you let me know?
 You think it might be?
 I don't know. Sometimes we seem to read each other's minds. Always. But she might have been dreaming.
 Can I ring you?
 Do that, she said.

He moved quietly into the room, a shift of light that had no shape, no edge. Moving about the basin, reflected briefly in the mirror, forming from the greyness, the flowers in his hands.
 The others are still fresh, she said.
 He looked up quickly. Jessica. I thought you were asleep. Yes, they are. They can go together.

You needn't bring them, Richard. Go to that trouble.
It's no trouble.
He sat by the bed. She was looking beyond him, to the wide stretch of sky, dark, the patterns of lights, lines of streets clear like a grid. The red glow along the curving highway. A giant video game, he said.
Video?
Down there. At night.
Is it night?
Yes. Now.
A nurse stood briefly in the doorway. Smiled at him. Kathy had perhaps been right. Beyond all this, now, a vagueness, always. Something not touched. Which he did not question, and he had always been comfortable with it. The two of them in silence.
Kathy in that nothing like her mother. Assertive. Driving the girls. Angry when he protested. But a talent. Lost to herself in those roles and scenes he had watched. At times with the girls, both of them, as he was, proud of her. If those images, those projections, were what she wanted. What she believed she could have done. What she believed, perhaps, she could still do. In the plane, pursuing some vision she despised. Or the steps to it despised. An ambition fading. It was difficult to know. Impossible. The woman's light cold fingers on his startling him.
You are tired.
No, he said.
You have been very good to me.
No. We have always been good company for one another.
Kathy will come?
Yes. Later.
The flowers were rich, massed on the glass shelf in the half light.
Her father. I want to say something to her.
I will tell her.

He was here, she said.

She should not have taken the window seat. Looking down. The plane banking for the low range of hills, not hills, a scarp, Richard always said, as it moved in air that could not hold and the ribs of land turned beneath them she was afraid. Trying to walk across a plank in the garden when she was a child. If you don't look down, her mother said. A swing, the plank across two drums, the patch of yellow sand by the fence. All the rest clean, tidy. The gardener every week. Sometimes an extra day. Thin, preoccupied, as if he might forget something, looking at them with a contempt she did not understand. Camellia bushes in the shade at the side of the house, the wide diamond shaped bed of roses at the front. The flowers strangely beautiful, touching the petals, the bushes higher than herself. Don't touch them, her mother said. The petals bruise.

The ground below now brown, bare. A few dark patches of scrub. A long black stain of fire, smoke drifting from the edges. All geometrical. Even. Circles of what might be water. The lines of dams. Mud coloured. But it is not like that, she said. It is, Richard said. From here. Leaning across, quickly. It's dead. All that area. It's surprising how much, I suppose. Going back to his paper. He did not like talking in planes. They're like public toilets, he said. She could not remember how long ago that had been.

Her mother standing by the wide glass doors to the terrace. The heat of the early afternoon. As if her mother allowed it, carefully, into the house. She said: Will you please listen to me. I am listening, Kathy. You don't hear. What am I saying? That you want to go on with your acting. I want to go to Sydney. Her mother looking at the tubs of greenery on the terrace. As if she calculated them. Measured. Yes. Sydney. I know you said that, Kathy. But you don't care, do you. Kathy, it doesn't matter if I care. How could it? But you don't think I should leave Richard. Her mother closed the doors quietly. The glass panels clean. Clear. I have thought you would. I like Richard. Yes you do. He should have married you. Before you say anything, that's a joke. Her mother said: And the girls? I'm so often over there they won't notice. That might be true, Kathy. But if you have to do this. You think I don't understand. Perhaps I do, much more than you realise. She said: We're not fighting. Nothing bitter. We'll manage it decently. It's not so bad. No, her mother said. I understand.

The land gone. The faint white ridges of the waves. Some vast piece of wrinkled cloth. A thought worthy of Terry. And that film. Islands. There were none down there. Terry with an undying fund of solid cliches. All of them workable. Most translated into moving images. With competence. Which people liked. And critics understood. The hostess beside her. She said: I'm sorry. I didn't realise. No. Nothing, thank you.

The woman's hand was relaxed. She was sleeping, but if he moved his own hand the thin fingers held a faint response. Jessica, he said. In his tiredness, the warm air, the quiet of the room, he might himself have slept. Beyond the windows the lights patterned the roads and buildings he did not recognise, shaped differently in darkness, each time to be placed again. The nurse came into the room, for a moment he had not seen her, she might have been watching them. She said: Asleep. If you want to leave.

She moved the woman's arm, straightened the cover. By

the door she said: She was talking to me before you came. I think she thought I was your wife. She wanted to tell me about someone in the war.

I see. And did she?

Well, in a way. I didn't understand. I thought in some way it was about you.

No, Richard said. It would not have been about me.

No. I realised. But it was very confused. And then she seemed to see me and she stopped. I mean, she realised I was not her daughter.

She didn't say who it was? Or what she wanted to tell Kathy? Her daughter.

She never mentioned any name.

No, he said. Thank you anyhow. And for all you're doing.

Along the walls of the corridors massive aboriginal art designs. Fusions of careful patterns of colour. Precise. Repetitive. He walked quickly. In the car park the lines of cars were shadowed, small trees, shrubs, breaking the ordered rows, suddenly strange in the darkness so that he stopped at the pavement, moved back.

The carp were still in the brown water, held by the clear light, and heat, they feel the warmth, she said, of course they do. And they are not gold. Red. A very fine red. The leaves of the waterlillies shadowing the water by the banks. Beyond the ponds trees screened the red brick buildings of the law courts. The lawns thinned about the exposed roots and patches of deep shade. He could no longer hear the city. Trams passing down Barrack Street to the ferry almost silent. The neatly wrapped lunch packet, the stiff white paper, opened easily. The carp barely moving.

She came towards him, along the path clear of shadow, towards the top of the steps above the ponds. She said: I thought you were asleep.

Barbara, he said.

You were expecting someone else?

Watching the carp, he said. But it was Kant's fault.

Kant.

His blue spectacles. And that pond.

You should give up that class. I don't see you as a philosopher.

Too late now.

She opened the paper bag she had carried. Actually I don't see the problem. I accept if you're born with blue spectacles the world looks blue.

Is blue.

Looks. And I accept you have to learn that it isn't. Word games.

No, he said. But you write my essay. Her features strong, the clear white skin, the fine dark brows he had traced with his fingers. The full lips she held firmly. Her dark hair, worn rather long, in a roll on her neck, not quite to her shoulders. At times impatient, I'm going to cut all this. I can't be bothered with it.

She said: Well?

Nothing, he said. Just looking. In fact I was wondering what you'd look like with a pair of blue glasses.

Oh, I wear them all the time.

She had taken a small salad roll from the bag, and a heavy chocolate eclair.

How you eat that, he said. In the middle of the day.

Hungry. And I don't have a loving aunt to give me lunch every day.

Not loving, he said. I doubt she has ever loved anyone.

That's rather sad.

No. No, it's not. She reminds me of some tribal flock. Or an armed pack. No private feeling, but a strong sense of the clan. The family.

That was never one of my worries.

I have this essay, he said. For this afternoon. Somehow. But the beach. Tomorrow?

We could stay. This weather. Yes.

I'm reading a book. And that gets in the way of the essay. Perth in the depression. It was banned. Joe Messer lent it to me. *Upsurge*.

Your friend the communist.

What does that mean?

Joe Messer. He is a communist.

Yes he is.

And he'd like you to be.

If I want to be.

It's too good a day to argue, she said. You reform the world if you want to.

And you don't care. As an artist, why don't you care?

A would be artist, she said. I care. But I'm not stupid enough to think you and I can do it. Or that it can be done at all from here.

The carp moved slowly, without effort, in the brown water, the heavy bodies touching. Their mouths moving. A kind of rhythm, he said. Like singing. Quietly.

They're beautiful. I might draw them.

They eat their spawn. What a lot of trouble that would save.

I'm going, she said. The old bat doesn't like me being away at lunch time.

You have to have a lunch hour.

Not where I work.

He stood beside her, his hand touching her arm, white, firm, the sleeve to her elbow, and she said: Saturday.

The market gardens held along the road, beyond the low swampland, drained and dry, marked by low grey scrub, the few trees. The stiff clumps of rush thick by the sides of the road, each summer burned, thinning. Rows of green, and the yellow lines of sand, the grey of the swamp soil. The few suburban houses displaced, iron sheds, the long streaks and splashes of rust. The fields of Arles, she said. Not those where the land itself writhed. Those with the clear spaces of yellow and green. A landscape of paper, of books, sudden unexpected illustrations. Travelling a hardly known landscape, perhaps by bus. Like this. Some place to stay. Houses, the cottages that might not be changed. She turned towards him, but he was looking ahead, as if he watched the road, and she did not speak. He

said suddenly: Those carp in the gardens. Yesterday.
  Why them?
  What do you think they saw?
  Looking up?
  Yes.
  A world upside down, maybe. Why? Didn't your essay come out?
  Yes. In a way. It's odd, I want to do well in philosophy, but I have more trouble getting a clear essay together than in any other subject.
  Not odd at all. Surely the whole idea is not to be clear.
  Go back to sleep, he said. We're nearly there. I'll wake you.
  Not asleep.
  Where were you?
  Arles, she said.
  He took the small case and roll of rugs. To the north the sweep of beach drew away to the far point. The beach deserted. The corner shop empty. They bought a drink at the milk bar and the man went back into the room behind the counter. The broken white road followed the edge of the rocks, the line of small cliffs. Where the limestone ended they walked down to the curve of beach, the dark line of weed banks. Small flies rose from the weed.
  It will be rotten in a month, he said. It smells enough now.
  The winter takes it away.
  And brings it back. Always just here.
  The road ended near a small cleared space, edged by rushes and a few wattles. A low broken rock wall. Sorrento, he said. I don't know why they call it that. Or what happened to it.
  It never was, she said. Or perhaps everyone just went away. I'm taking my shoes off. I can't walk in the sand.
  Beyond the first of the high dunes they turned in along a narrow eroded cleft, the sand shifting.

The sand, she said. It's steeper. No wonder they abandoned this place.

From the top of the dune the thick wattle scrub held against the slope, a green surface below them, she let her feet slide, the sand in a wide spray. At the base, the small space in the wattle, shadowed, it's like a rock cave, she said, and they had worked to clear the ground. The bed of dead wattle leaves and small boughs on the sand, the two planks that made a table. The sand crossed by thin lines of tracks. She said: The lizards have been busy.

In the cleared space she put down the paint box, the few parcels. They found the scraps we left. I'm tired. It was further today.

The dunes move, he said. Who knows.

She walked along the wash of the small waves, the water almost flat, there was no wind and he swam slowly just beyond the darker line of deepening water. She would hesitate, wading in the shallow, crying out at the cold, then suddenly throw herself to swim out towards him. Strongly, often faster than he was. Staying longer in the water. The long afternoons at City Beach, in mid summer, where they swam idly, catching the few waves big enough to break over them, time drawn in to the sun and the water and the light, until their skin seemed taut and their fingers puckered from the water and from cold. If you won't come in, he said, it will be dark.

The fire reflected from the iron, the back and curving sides of the fireplace. The flames lifted slowly against the blackened metal. Black, and reflecting. You are dreaming, he said.

No. A technical problem. The way the flames are. The light.

Did you hear what I was saying?

Not really.

No. I was trying to say it is the only book that has told the truth. A part of the truth. No one has wanted to write about that early part of the depression.

No one has wanted to read about it.

That, yes. There's a scene describing the riot outside the Treasury. I had just started at the bank. I knew there was trouble down there. There'd been rumours all day. I was going out with the mail, but they found an excuse and I couldn't go. They sat there and worked at their pieces of paper and counted their coins and notes. Some of the men spoke to one another as if they were afraid someone would hear. I think they really believed the unemployed were going to take over the streets of Perth. Wreck all the banks and offices along the Terrace.

Well they didn't do that.

They didn't do anything. A few pickets ripped off the fence along the Supreme Court Gardens. Where we have lunch. And no one remembers what happened. No, they didn't do anything.

The title is a bit odd.

Upsurge? A bit ironic.

We were always very well behaved here, she said. Maybe we always are. I don't know that I mind that.

The book got itself banned. And Harcourt went over East. I suppose he had to get out.

Maybe we all do.

But he didn't care much about hiding his characters. I know who he means by the judge when the unemployed were tried in court. And the shop owner where one of the girls worked. I wouldn't say much had changed there. He was always after women. And the chemist.

Well, tell me.

You can read it. But it's like the Americans. Hard. Honest.

The way you want to write.

The way I think I have to write.

Hurry up and finish it.

The dry thin wood burned quickly, a fine ash, darkening about the faint colour. She lay close to him, the rug about them. She said: Did you write this week?

Something. Between essays. But it's not going to be what I want.

Put it aside. You could come with me.

I write out of here. I have to.

No one knows we exist. The rest of the world.

Not important.

Of course it is.

This is what matters.

Your way, she said, there's nowhere else. We should both go.

He woke in the night, and she was turned towards him, her head against his shoulder. She breathed easily, comfortable, and he did not move. There was no wind, the slow infrequent break of the waves clear, sharp. The dark wattle still, if one of the long seed pods dropped he would hear it. She had sketched the pods, the long brittle curve, ridged, the round cups and the small black seeds. With a minute wing of orange-yellow. Very exact. You should illustrate text books, he said. There was no moon. Hardly the outline of the dunes. Rain. Camping at Scarborough, when he was still at the bank, the few days holidays measured out. Rain coming suddenly through the thin stand of trees. He had not known her then. In the small city they could not have been so far from one another. The bank. All over the city men put off as they reached an adult wage. Or had reached one. A time of youth. A time for some. If you leave now you will not find another job, his mother said. And in the day the surf and the heavy boards, at night the amusement park on the promenade, the loudspeaker. *Stormy Weather. Remember My Forgotten Man.* The singer's voice. Words lost in the harsh

31

amplifiers. And the wind. Blown along the dark beach.

It's so far from anywhere, she said. Or maybe it isn't anywhere.

She balanced the block on her knees. The long-sleeved blouse over her bathers, her firm white legs bare, the sun always burned her. I'm a freak in this climate. A goanna, he said. One of the lizards round the camp. You shed your skin. Lying on the beach while he smoothed oil over her shoulders, her back. You can go on doing that, she said. She drew firmly, decisively, often her drawing stark, without compromise, but there could be a delicacy that surprised him. And disturbed him, patterned as he would have had words patterned.

This place has kept itself, he said. The beach this morning. Clean, even where we walked yesterday there's no sign.

No one has ever been here.

I wish that was true.

It is, she said. This morning. Her hand moved quickly above the paper. Perhaps it always will be.

Do you want to draw this? He held the cuttleshell so that it caught the light, white, and the dark crescent lines, the faint rim of red that would fade.

Yes, she said. To make it fill a frame. Nothing else. Just that white curve, like the dunes really, and those markings. Very big. No one will know what it is.

It won't be anything by then.

Right. One of my despised abstracts.

It's too easy being a painter, he said. She did not answer, and he said: Do you still get anything from your art classes?

Not much. I've got all I can now.

But you still go there.

Practice. I keep in touch. See other students. Like you at University.

I'm not sure other students help.

The hard lines of the dunes, the tracery of bushes, salt plants, long flowing exposed roots where the wind had cut gullies in the dunes. The ripples of sand.

You draw so easily, he said. And well.

A few thin clouds held along the far point, the clear curve of beach.

All this, he said. Somehow I want to get this. It has to be part. But I don't know how to do it. It's simply that much harder in writing.

Movies, she said. One day. Perhaps.

Now is not one day. You can get it down, like you do there. But I can't make it take shape.

It's not all I want to do, she said. There has to be a lot more than this.

But this is part of it.

For you.

Yes. So you have to go away.

Yes.

It doesn't make sense.

It has to. You could come.

You've finished that, he said. We can swim.

She put the block on the sand, the box of pencils across it, covered them with her towel. He drew the thin blouse up over her head, her arms lifting. He touched her shoulders.

You won't need your bathers. No one will come here this weekend. And you won't burn with this sun.

Let me draw you first. There at the edge.

You've put your things away.

They can be unput. Now.

He stood where she pointed, the waves breaking out beyond him, the thin wash running at his feet. Hurry, he said.

All right now, she said. He looked at the quickly lined pieces of body, arms, legs angled at the wash.

All bits and pieces. Art class.
She put the block down. It will come together.

The cloud streamers lifted above the dunes, gold, deep red. Fading. The colour of the flames. In the small pan the two pieces of meat were red, browning, the white edges of fat colouring, the darker lines. He moved the pan slowly. At the plank table she sliced the tomatoes and the last of the bread on the two plates.

At school, she said, we used to draw things like this. Apples. Fruit.

You were good at it. Don't tell me.

Yes. I had a drawing book and every page had a merit stamp on it. I was proud of that. She watched him outlined against the flame of the small fire, intent, at ease. Strange really.

Strange? Being proud of your work? Or drawing things in school. Yes, that is strange, I suppose.

You. The fire.

It will be the late bus. No point in trying to go early.

You can climb your mulberry tree.

Tonight, he said, the front door.

The old tree shadowed the side of the house, heavy against the walls and over the roof. In winter, with the wind from the river hardly broken by the thin line of rushes and paperbarks, its boughs beating at the iron. I don't see how you can sleep, she said, and he laughed. It's natural. A part of things. She had not at first believed him about climbing the heavy bough that forked below the window, to get into his room at night. But surely your aunt can't object, she said. You're making it up. No, he said. Not object. She doesn't say anything about what I do. I don't think she cares. She just wants to know. Know what? It's crazy. Yes, it is. Know when I come in. I think she lies awake. Or maybe never sleeps. Why not let her then, she said. I expect she's lonely. About that, he said, no. I doubt she knows the meaning of that word. It's a kind of spying. For her own satisfaction. I think it annoys her if she can't be sure when I come in. If she fell asleep, or missed the door. She's a part of the house. What happens to it happens to her. A door. A window opening. Someone walking. No. I don't want to annoy her. We get on all right. I just don't want to be spied on, be absorbed by the house. No.

Your mulberry tree, she said. Perhaps I don't believe it.

She knew he had gone there when he started work in the city, as a family arrangement, his wage from the bank would not have kept him. Now he stayed there because he had a room where he could work and not be disturbed. And she believed because there was an odd tension between him and the elderly woman she had met only twice. The first time when he showed her the mulberry tree. Just to prove it is there, he said. The tree was heavy with dark fruit, the berries staining their fingers and lips as she ate and he picked some for her to take home. I should throw them down at you, he said. It's like Lawrence. You don't throw those, she said. And it's not like that with us. God no, he said. Nothing further. But it's a wonderful book. The soft fruit staining her mouth. Would you write like that? No, I don't think I could. Seaforth Mackenzie that I showed you, that's Lawrence. Part of it, I suppose, she said. But I don't think of it like that.

This is a fine meal, she said. It's as well we can never carry much out here.

She had given him a drawing of the mulberry tree, very dark, strong against the house, the shadowed bricks of the wall, to give to his aunt, but she did not know if he had.

When they had packed the things he put the scraps on a clear patch of sand near the base of the dune.

They'll have to hurry, she said. It will be too dark. Do they move about at night?

They might if it's warm enough.
It's not. Not tonight. Is it?
I don't know. The morning will be time. You could stay here and guard it.
Yes I could, she said. Why don't I.

In the darkness the white lines of surf ran clearly, and there were the few distant lights to the south. Where the beach ended, the broken limestone above them, the lights were hidden. Waves threw a fine spray from the rock. They could hear the wind.
Where we climb, he said. And it's dark.
Seamen off some old ship, she said. Castaways. I can hear them.
From the road the lights made a broken pattern ahead, they walked on the sides of the white track, the ruts smoothed, the white crown of raised stone between them. She stumbled, bumping against him, and he held her arm. She said: Maybe we should buy a boat.
He had taken a desk near hers, late, the adult education lecture filling the room, the lecturer opening his book. Watching her as the lecture moved among the Victorians and Thomas Hardy, and through the reading of the last scene of *Tess* she sat quite still, her lips moving as if she followed the words. Knowing suddenly she was close to tears, and the reader's voice deep, slow. People moving, standing, the scrape of chairs, she looked at him and he said: I don't know how he reads like that. Surprised he had spoken. It was wonderful, she said. They walked along the colonnade to wait for the trolley bus. She said: I sat up all night reading *Jude*. I cried. I looked terrible when I went to work. The woman I work for asked had someone died. I said yes. The bus swayed at the wide curves of the road that bordered the river. I've never heard anyone read like that, she said. I knew that was how it should be. At the Esplanade he looked at the lighted street, the thin, clipped

hedge of the Weld Club a dull green, the pavement shadowed. He touched the leaves of the hedge. Dust. What do you expect, she said. In the small cafe, along the half lit arcade, the waitress took their order, brought them coffee and toast. She's tired, the girl said. He looked at the grey, empty arcade. She said: I like these night lectures. Yes, he said. Though I wish they would come out of the past. Something on the modern Americans. Forward, not past. She looked up quickly. Backwards is important. He raised his hands. But so is now. No one down there reads the modern Americans. And no one reads Australian work. She filled their cups from the small coffee pot. You mean at the University? Are you there? I suppose you could say that is where I am, he said. She laughed. I'm sorry. I know what you mean about the past. I try to paint. But it does mean you have something ahead. Somewhere to go. Where there's room. Yes, he said. If you can find the way. I know about that, too, she said. She looked at the last fingers of toast, brown, limp. If you don't want that? I don't have time to eat, the nights I go to adult lectures. We could have something more, he said. She looked at the girl behind the counter. Not here. They want to close up. In the empty street, clear of parked cars, traffic, he walked with her to the Town Hall, she caught a tram for West Perth, and he walked down to the ferry. Beyond the lighted waiting room the lamps made arcs on the grey planking of the jetty.

From the limestone road the wind was stronger. If the bus has gone, she said, I'm not walking back.

For a moment he saw her clearly, then the tram moving up Barrack Street halted at the intersection. He crossed behind the tram. She was standing by the lighted shops of the Town Hall, looking across the street at the Franceska Bookshop window as if she read the titles, the patterns of the bright dust jackets, unaware of the people, the cars slowing to the intersection, the trams. Noise. Her plain black dress, long sleeved, the colour of her hair, almost. Trying one morning in a lecture he no longer heard to describe her, a page, rewritten. He kept it, then showed her. Perhaps it's true, she said. Some bits are. But kind. Thanks. It's not meant to be kind, he said. He stepped up onto the pavement, the cars held briefly at the intersection.

You look very striking. Standing there. Against the window.

Something for your writing.

No.

She walked easily beside him. You look tired.

Fighting an essay. I was reading late.

Overtime. Like your bank.

Overtime was part of the job.

Why did you hate it so much?

I'm not sure it was hate. My family got me the job. Everyone saying how lucky I was when there were no jobs. A few jobs for underpaid juniors, they meant. It got me away from the country, I suppose I thought I could work at that and have interests outside. But it wasn't going to be like that. I just couldn't stand it. Inside those walls. My family were good about it.

Perhaps you'd have made a good banker.

Become an adviser to the government. Some of them were. Don't laugh.

It's not funny. There's something sad in people like your friend who thinks they've got the promised land if they can change the government.

He has faith.

I had an uncle once. He had faith. He was in the Salvation Army. I used to sit on his knee and he felt my bottom.

A wise man. We might see him tonight. They play on the corner near the Hall.

Uncle's trying his hand with the cherubs now. Very accessible. Maybe the odd angel.

What did you do about it?

I didn't do anything. It was rather nice, actually.

Randy bitch. But Joe believes in this theatre group. That can't be bad.

I don't think I believe in him. If it comes to believing in things.

He's very involved. It all matters to him. It's not easy being a communist in this place.

I won't say why be one. I prefer your boxer friend.

Harry believes in himself. Even when he loses.

I'd like to be like that. I'm not sure if I could be. When I'd lost.

You won't lose, Barbara.

Thanks, she said. If you mean it. Does he lose often?

About even. He won over four rounds last week. He's going up.

And he lives like that.

Some of them try. He's got a sideline. He's a kind of runner. And he's at the wharves a lot. A mover. I don't say what he moves comes from the wharves. I don't know where it comes from. Anywhere, probably.

Moving what?

You'd have to ask him that. It's not official.

I'll come with you one night and see him fight.

You'd create a sensation at the Unity.

It would be something to draw. I'm serious.

No, he said. Go to the wrestling. Some women go there.

If you'll take me.

We can try. And if you walk across the road like that you won't go anywhere.

Thinking of Harry. All those muscles.

He said: You are a randy bitch.

Inside the Assembly Hall he said: Actually this place is not too different from the stadium. You could put a ring up on the stage. Bring it forward a bit.

I didn't mean to start this, she said. We came to see a play.

The first play started abruptly, people still in the aisles, talking, then members of the cast moving from among them, the unexpectedness carrying to the bare stage, the few effects, the sudden energy and humour, the play riding hard its social satire. At the interval she said: I don't see your friend.

He's in *Waiting For Lefty*. At a guess I'd say he was back there trying to learn his lines.

He'd have no trouble improvising.

Prejudice, he said. Do you ever think of designing sets? Interiors, backgrounds for plays?

No.

Why not?

I don't know why not. Messy, I think. People everywhere.

You are very self sufficient.

You don't write plays.

The hall darkened, to the bare stage, the semi circle of men, seated, the gunman by the door. The light fading and the men in shadow, the spotlight centre of the stage and the couple in the first of the episodes. The play moving to strength and conviction, a raw force, the episodes forming from the light and shadow, the group of men half hidden, the centre stage clear, the rise to tension and at the end the lighted space of the stage filling with the presence of the men, arms lifted, voices shouting in belief.

In the street the shop windows caught the light of cars, the buildings dark. He said: I've never seen anything like that. And how can it be here. How could you write that.

It reminds me of *Upsurge*.

In a way. There was something here. For someone to

get. I think it's impossible now.
 Whatever there was there's no way that play could have come out of it.
 There has to be.
 You'll have to come with me. Not wait for something that's not there.
 We come back to this, he said. And it's not an answer.
 The gate a dark gap in the fence overgrown by pittosforum, the white flowers in the late summer sweet scented, heavy, the veranda enclosed by the climbing rose that twisted about the roof, all wood, his aunt said, it will never flower. Forming, above the single step, another gap to the front door. The house dark. The door opened quietly to the narrow tunnel of the passage, where he had no need of the light, finding the door to his room. The darkness of the tree about the window. For a time, his hands on the wide board sill, he looked into the darkness, the lighter shapes of shadow on what had been the lawn.

He did not know how old the house was. His aunt vague, she and her husband had bought it just before the war, his parents claimed, she never spoke directly of her marriage. It had been built and sold by someone who liked the position close to the river, in South Perth, but had discovered that in a wet winter the river rose above the narrow strip of beach, through the reed beds, and washed close to the side fence. The house fronted the street so that the river could only be seen through the kitchen window. Or, before the day of the climbing rose, from the front veranda. The water seeped about the garden, where the ground sloped behind the mulberry tree it formed a long pond where there were frogs, and once he had seen a blue crane stalking the shallow stretch of water. A garden intended as a show piece, the creation and interest of his uncle, if the term could be applied to such a circuitous relationship. What did happen to your uncle, Barbara said. He did not answer until he had picked the mulberries and stood beside her in the heavy shade of the tree. This place has ears. It listens. I'm not sure it doesn't talk. I'll tell you later. On the ferry as they went back to the city, the water still and dark as if without depth, she said: Well? What did happen? He watched the even furrow that spread towards the posts marking the channel, washing suddenly in small waves at the shallows. He said: Low tide. What happened was he fell down the back steps one night. On his way to the loo. I see, she said. You'd better be careful. I am. But it wasn't as simple as that. He was still there next morning. When he was found. A heavy man. My aunt could not have moved him. He had another problem, apart from the garden. He drank. That's what the family always called it. Just two words. To them it said everything. Officially that's what happened. I don't think I like that, she said. Doesn't it, I don't know, disturb you? Being there? The place is harmless, he said.

Overtaken now by the garden. Bamboos sending their green spears through the damp soil about the back fence. An increasing thicket, polished lances and the high plumes of a waiting troop. Old creepers heavy about a spare jarrah, its upper branches dead. Clumps of arum lillies and agapanthus. In the summer there were snakes but no one went so far into the yard and his aunt once said they ate the frogs. I don't know why you ever went there, Barbara said. You could get a room out in West Perth. No river or snakes. At least I haven't seen any. No cheap rents either, he said. But I told you, I had to live there when I started at the bank. It's that I didn't like. I don't care what the house is, but I live with a relative, my family were responsible for the job in the bank, they were willing to help me give it up to go to the university. I go back up there to the farm to work over harvest if they need me. It's all family. She said: But that makes sense. You could be like me. My family don't want to know. That could be better, he said. His aunt made no demands, so selfcontained she in a way excluded him. Gave him the large quiet room where he could work, spread books and papers, leave manuscript, and was never disturbed. One convention was established, without words so that he was not sure how it had come about, at meals she would talk to him, and he was to have his meals in the wide room off the kitchen at the back of the house. With her. If he was to be out she liked to know. She talked, then, at times of the news, but mostly of the city in its earlier period, of family relationships, of what she called the north, where she had been as a young girl. Where some of his relatives established the first sheep run. Or so it seemed. It was not something his own parents spoke of, and he never asked them. A past recaptured, recaptured at second and third hand, from fragments she had welded to her own experience. When the river rose about the house the previous winter she told him of great floods in the north, houses washed away, miles of land under water, the work of the men rescuing people isolated on small pieces of land, clinging to roof tops, some swept away in the first night of the rising water. It would have been irreverent to ask did she think they might, the two of them, have to climb onto the roof of this suburban house as the water rose about the garden. Washed away through the drowning suburbs.

And she talked to herself, in the house. He heard her. To herself, or whoever, or whatever, shared those rooms, that long passage way. At times she might simply have shifted her voice to pitch it from herself to him, as if he was not there for her at all. At night she listened to the wireless, its rounded shining cabinet set by itself on a small table in the front room. The voices quiet, unassertive. She might have talked to it. Speaking of the past. Turning the other voices backward. Everything's the past, he said. What people did. What the State did. How it all got started here. The past.

Statues guarded the entrance, solid white torsos, arms upraised, their sightless eyes. Greek. Victorian. Copies, she said. Though they have been here long enough to be original.

They turned right to the long gallery. To the left stairs led down to endless bottles of fish, preserved in slightly brown liquid. What would happen, he said, if a visitor was looking for the art gallery and got down there? It's just that it would be more interesting, she said.

The gallery was quiet, a clear light from the high ceiling. The long walls of paintings. Hung carefully. Spaced. For size, she said. One of the students said this was a barn. A kind of cow shed. But the truth is I realised I don't know what other galleries are like. Only from pictures and art books.

Would you be very disappointed if they were all the same?

I'd die.

You are putting a lot on the line.

Yes, she said. Everything.

There were few people in the gallery, a couple with children held back from the walls, a small group she said had to be tourists. A boat in and with nothing to do on a Sunday afternoon. He said: Harry claims the boats try to be out of port by Sundays, to dodge the rates.

Harry ducking, weaving his way through three rounds, an elusive fighter, exploding suddenly to life near the end of the last round, a tactic that often enough shocked a tired opponent. And brought him the crowd. It's the finish, he said. It's all in the finish. After the fight going down Roe Street to the small house where French Rene worked. Come down there, he said. They're good to me there. I might take French out of it one day. If there's some bloody where to take her.

To dodge this city on a Sunday, you mean, she said. What are you thinking about? You were lost.

A girl called French Rene. I think I'm tired of these paintings.

People got tired of them a long time ago. They've been here forever. They make your point about the past, I suppose.

You're going to the past.

These are just bad past. What I'm against is not all this stuff, but recreating it. Allowing nothing else.

About that, he said, we agree. But in here, what do the gallery people do all day?

Perhaps they dust these things. Occasionally. Not enough to disturb them.

Let's go up to your place, he said. At least no one dusts that.

She pushed him suddenly, so that he swung sideways, the children looking towards him. They want a fight, he said.

She stood before the large painting near the end of the right wall. I came to look at this. Then we'll go.

Strong in the foreground the couple, man and woman, bound, stripped to the waist, behind them their people, a line, lust in the faces, lust transformed in punishment. Made respectable. Perhaps not lust. Simply cruelty. Needing little respectability.

I thought gypsies were very tolerant about this kind of thing, he said. All the books I've read have the women as very dangerous.

It was dangerous for these two. It's probably a matter of

being found out.

The painting was a seven day's wonder here. People from everywhere that had never been inside the gallery.

And because no one could remember when we had a new picture here.

It does have some nice erotic suggestions. We're not used to this kind of thing.

I wanted to look at the technique, she said. For something I'm doing. But I should have known. Flint has his own skills. But it's no use to me. All right. We'll go.

He lay on the bed, the sheet heaped on the floor, their clothes on a chair. The room shadowed, the curtains of the window that opened to the half enclosed verandah drawn. On the end of the table her sketching pads and a box of colours, two stained glass jars of water, on the bare wood she set cups and the tea pot. Space, she said. One day I'll have a studio.

One day we might have a house.

Do you think so?

No.

No. But I don't care about that.

I don't care about that either. What I would like is to be with you in some decent place just for a while. Say a week.

All we'd last, she said. But yes, I'd like that. Still, we have the beach.

She took the cup of tea to him, her loose robe open, and he said: It would be better to be a painter. I could draw you. I can't get the same sort of thing in words. And if I could I wouldn't get it published. How you look now. Exactly. But all our writing is sterile. Plain bloody sterile.

The painting is something like that. Though you can do nudes. But it's like being in that gallery. I just feel I've got to get out. There has to be something different.

Somewhere else. You mean England. Europe.

There. Yes.

Half Europe is an armed camp. Or worse. You can't go there.

It's still possible. And England.

What would you do if you get caught in a war?

I don't know. She took his cup and put it by hers, filled them from the plain brown pot. I don't know. What would you do?

On the partition wall she had pinned some of her work, a nude study of him, side on, staring out the window. It's not that big, he said, and she laughed. Must be wishful thinking. Charcoal studies of groups of trees, two watercolours of the beach, the dunes, waves and sky fused to long bands of colour. No one likes that, she said. She told him the woman who let the room came in when she was out. Must be to look at you. Why don't you complain, he said. The old bag. I don't mind sharing you, she said.

I won't be caught in any European war, he said. I'd have nothing to do with that.

Her hand lay on her heavy white thigh, her fingers moving slowly over her own flesh. He reached out, his hand covering hers.

Your skin is cool. No. I'm not going to have any part in a war.

You're very sure.

My uncle, he said. Perhaps. More family if you like. When I was a child I saw what they brought home of him from a war. I dreamed of it for years. If that's what people want to do to one another, no. And the terrible thing, the thing I must have realised even then, is that he wanted to live. Even like that he wanted to live.

Her hand turned, holding his, forcing it against her. He said: Neither he nor my father or anyone else in those years believed it had achieved anything. They didn't think there would be no more war. They believed there would be another war.

They seem to have been right.

For a lot of them that didn't seem to matter. The best years. Like the red page of the *Western Mail*. It's an old boys' club. Chatty anecdotes about the war. Remembrance of things past. Things loved. Those things. Nothing else.

And your uncle?

He did die. And I felt glad because I didn't have to see him any more. I was guilty about that for bloody years.

She took the cups and put them on the table. The water in one of the jars beside them was a deep brown, sharp suddenly against the white cup. She slipped the robe from her shoulders and it fell across the dark square of carpet. He moved for her on the narrow bed. She said: I'm sorry.

Someone called it an English village, he said. You should be warned.

The buildings were held by the curve of the river, rising with the slight lift of the land, beyond them the line of hills. A stillness. The light fixed.

Where everyone takes photographs, she said. All the views are from King's Park. And it is nice to look down on it like this. But it reminds me of our exhibitions, I don't know, Johnson, Powell, all the rest, people say how good and there is a technique, in a way, yes. But there's this kind of glaze. Like the light down there. Everything has halted.

Well, it has.

And if you want an alternative, what is there. Social realism.

That didn't exactly harm American writing, he said.

It mightn't harm our painting. It just doesn't attract me. I might be more interested in surrealism if I knew more about it.

You are surreal. But it's not something this town offers any welcome to.

I won't be in this town.

You keep reminding me, he said. Maybe I can find you a different view. The old man wants to see me over Easter. I think he's worried about this war business and what will happen.

What will happen?

I think he feels there's likely to be no labour. Though the price of wheat might rise. Ironic. But it would be different to looking down at Perth and the river. Thomas Wolfe wrote a book called *Of Time And The River*. I wish I'd thought of the title.

Could you have written the book?

Since you mention it, no.

But Easter, she said. I thought we were going to the beach.

Yes. But you could come up there.

How would I do that?

You get in the train. If you've never been that far on the government railways it's an experience you should have. Leave Thursday.

Are you serious?

You'd be welcome. All those lovely gum trees you could draw. Paint, if you want to bring your gear.

I just might, she said. Except I have to work Thursday. I'd have to take a sickie.

Take it.

You don't care if I lose my job.

You're going to England. You can't take it with you. Seven thirty-five Thursday morning. If the crew on the last leg are sober we should be there about four o'clock.

The carriage was full to Northam. He edged in quickly for a window seat, and she watched the trees, the cuttings as the line rose into the scarp, the colours of the faces of the stone, the few clearings dry at the end of summer. They did not talk. He bought her a cup of tea at Chidlows, the bell tolling on the station platform.

I've never been further than this, she said. Beyond Northam. And here only once.

It's where the world begins.

At midday they had the carriage to themselves. They ate the sandwiches his aunt had packed. She refused to open those she had brought, cut hurriedly that morning.

They're terrible, she said. But it was so early.

I said there was no need. My good aunt would never let me go home without proper provision. The disgrace.

We can leave them for something to eat out there. Are there things that would eat them?

End of summer, he said. Something might.

He lay with his head against her, and she watched the bare paddocks, the few stands of trees, patches of salt land.

I didn't know it was like this, she said.

It's a time capsule, this train. Only it doesn't get anywhere. In time. It's very weird. I've been trying to make sense of relativity. And Whitehead. I don't know. Perhaps we're not old enough. For a perspective. It's one thing to try to get an intellectual grip of something like relativity, but it's another to see it in some real way.

How do you see a mathematical formula in some real way?

All right. I suppose what I've been thinking about is in life. People. Events. I've been trying to read Proust, but I can't. I just keep putting it down. To come back to. What I mean is more like the Priestley play. At the Repertory Club. *Time And The Conways*.

Yes. What might have been. Or what was?

Choices. Different patterns in time. If we had choices.

Oh we do, she said.

You're more certain than I am.

And what I resent about time is how much of it I have to spend working in that place where I spend the day.

The land increasingly cleared, squares of fallow, land

grey with stubble and thin grass. Flat. Turning its own shifting horizon as the train moved. Without meaning. Without relation to anything she knew. The fields of Arles and the market gardens withered in distance. At the sidings a strange silence, the engine somewhere far from them. Perhaps gone. There is no one, she said. They have forgotten us.

One night they did do that, he said. The engine went on. Left the guard's van. The guard was full. He didn't know.

For a time she slept, and then he touched her shoulder and she looked up slowly and there was the small box of the siding and some motor trucks waiting on the cleared square behind it. A few trees and the curving bays of wheat bins. Dark shadow across the ground. Home, he said.

Those trees, she said. That I was going to draw. Where are they?

Someone must have cut them down.

I've never seen so much space. So much nothing.

Not nothing.

I don't think it's for me to draw. Or maybe understand. The outcamp is better.

The silence, she said. If I could draw that.

I tried to write about this. Silence. Space. A novel. Something like this place. A wheatcarter. A contract carrier. A woman. She was married. I think now it was the place I was trying to get. More than the people.

You never showed it to me.

I sent it to an agent in England. They gave me quite a fair report. It was too Australian. And needed a stronger plot.

You sent your novel to England, she said. But you won't go there yourself.

I thought about that. Yes.

And you don't think I should go there.

I didn't seem to have any alternative. I mean, most of the

books I read come from there, even the American writing has to be published there before us bloody colonials can see it. I read John O'Londons. Nash's Magazine. I think I was wrong now. By the time it came back I wanted to change it.

Did you?

No. And I think sending it there was a kind of romantic thing. England was where people could lead some kind of literary life, if you want to call it that. Where writing, publishing was going on. Where it seemed to have some importance. There's nothing of that here. But it's something I'm going to live with now.

It is not how I would solve it, she said.

The land sloped away gradually, and to the right she saw the outcamp. Low, earth walled, added to with galvanised iron, iron discoloured, stained, richly stained, the windows covered with iron. A new fence around it. Beyond the broken fallow, distant, the darkness of uncleared land against the horizon.

It was all like that once, he said. This was the old homestead. I used to wonder how the old man found his way. A day in to the siding. Back in the dark.

And you didn't like it.

I didn't mind that so much. No. Not as a child.

He opened the gate, took the utility through to one end of the building, by a tank stained with rust and damp. A greenness along the base, the stones of the support.

There is a tree, she said. One.

They put it in when the house was built. A pepper tree. There used to be a few of them on places round here. People planted them in the yards. I don't know why.

He sat by her in the shade, crushing the thin red skin from the hard berries of the tree, the scent sharp. She outlined the house, working more slowly than she usually did, finding shapes, the pattern of the rust and the discoloured timber. She said: Did you have your

discussion with your father?
　Not much to discuss. He was trying to find out what I might do, I think. I wasn't much help. I think they probably wanted a family reunion.
　They got a ring in.
　They like you. They'd be glad you came.
　Angles, small pieces, over and over some of the long stains of the iron, the small broken window, half shuttered. You're all bits and pieces, he said.
　I'm not going to see this again. I need to remember it. Why did you leave here?
　I'm not sure. It's not something I've much wanted to think about.
　I realised that. I'm sorry. It's just being here made me ask.
　I was afraid, in a way. He looked at the red berries in his hand, their husks curved, minute, the hard green centres. Afraid of all this. Of never getting away. Never getting away if I wanted to. You get involved. But all this is a kind of battlefield. It's broken enough people. You just fight the land. And look at it. I'm not sure it's not being destroyed. The timber gone. The salt spreading on the flats. Dust storms. I feel strongly for this country. I don't want to work at a kind of destruction.
　I can understand that, she said. If that is how it seems. And there is a sense of that. Destruction. I could feel it just looking from the train. I think it frightened me.
　Of course my people don't see it that way. Nor others. You end up being the odd man out. In all sorts of ways. That you killed things. Well, things to eat, to sell. It sounds trite enough. But I began to feel I couldn't do that. When I was old enough and was expected to. I think it all came to a point when I saw a new man we had, he didn't have any experience, he must have lied to my father about knowing farm work. He had to kill a calf, meat for the house, no waste in those days. He had to cut its throat and

he started and then he couldn't do it. The thing got away. I can still remember that. My father had to catch it and finish the job. I know that seems childish. And doesn't have anything to do with the real world.

She said: That's the point, isn't it. Adults are not likely to start caring about a calf with its throat half ripped open.

There was a lot of bitterness in the family before they realised I wasn't going to fit. It's odd, I haven't told anyone about that before. I used to dream about it. That calf trying to run and I stood there. It's very naive. Sorry. Maybe this visit wasn't such a good idea.

She took one of the longer sheets of paper, and pinned it to the board. She worked carefully, tentative, then with sudden force. She said: I knew a man was a vegetarian, once. People used to laugh at him. A crank.

I'm not sure I understand.

Wouldn't that follow from what you say.

I suppose it would. If you force it to that.

You eat meat. We enjoy it, cooking at the beach.

I know I eat meat. I'm just trying to tell you how all this seemed to me. That was part of a whole thing. It's not an argument.

No. I'm sorry.

You don't really understand, do you.

I think I do.

You're probably stronger than I am. Let it go. We can have lunch inside. I'll clean it up a bit.

He pushed open the door, and looked at the dust on the table, wiping it with a rag from a shelf near the fireplace.

Dust doesn't matter, she said.

This much does. It would grow a crop. Was he your lover?

My lover?

The vegetarian.

No. I didn't actually like him.

He dusted the chairs, old, straight backed. She spread

the lunch on the serviettes and paper wrappers his mother had packed.

All right, he said. Don't say it. Meat.

She held him to her suddenly, his face against the warm dress, faintly scented, and she said: Afterwards. I'm hungry. All this distance and silence.

Someone might come.

Here? No one will come here.

She placed her dress carefully over the back of the chair, moving slowly, as if she did not believe him. As at times she would wait, unwilling to throw her dress, a blouse or shirt, behind her and run across the sand. There are no spies in the dunes, he said, and once free, the waves before them, forgot. She turned to him and their bodies held and she guided him into her, standing, for a moment they did not move, then, separating slowly, lay on the pile of sacks stacked on the floor. No bed, she said. What has been in those? Their sweat picking up the sharp dust, itching. Perhaps we shouldn't have done this. Her heavy firm breasts that she brushed with her hand, a thin sweat, and he mouthed clean, then looked at her. You taste. She laughed, her shoulders quivering. Clean me all over if you like. You are strong, he said. Your body is beautiful, but she turned her head. No. But I don't care. Very black and white, he said, you could be your own model.

He went out to the tank by the broken verandah boards, and called her. She stood in the doorway, and he lifted the half fuel drum so that water slid slowly over his head and body, the runnels widening, slopping across the dark ground.

Yes. One of your better ideas. She gasped at the water. It's not cold. Wonderful.

If you don't look in the tank, he said.

She stood while he refilled the drum, running the tepid water slowly over her. What do you mean?

Things fall in. Do you want to look?

No. They stood in the sun on the verandah boards, the wood twisted, planks missing, she traced the strong forms and knots of the wood with her foot. She said: Like the quiet. And the light. Hard. Clear.

The main rooms of the house, the sitting room, his aunt's phrase, it was in fact where she sat in the evenings, her bedroom opposite, his own room, opened off the central passage, a dark lane crowded by an old umbrella and hat stand, a blue and white vase that held two walking sticks, a long cedar chest. A heavy plush curtain, deep red, held the end of the passage, behind it a wide dining room, again his aunt's description, a view of the bamboos, the creeper over the workshop and lavatory, the old jarrah. At one end of the dining room the door to the kitchen, at the other a bathroom. The room itself had once been sunlit, designed to offer a view of the garden. Now the garden, the curtains, old furniture, the deep red curtain of the passageway, took the light, the warmth. A cold room, one he did not like, but where each meal time he and his aunt sat at the heavy mahogany table. A table polished to a lustre, always with a clean table cloth for meals. His aunt could emerge from either part of the house, front or back, to stand before the red curtain with no disturbance of its heavy folds. A conjurer before a backdrop, surveying an audience. One night, in the splendour of the Ambassadors Cinema in Hay Street, as the vast red curtain parted, he said: I never believe in that thing. The curtain? Barbara said. Yes. We have one of those in South Perth.

Your friend, his aunt said. Called.

Barbara?

A man. He left a message.

I see.

He said Harry. He would be at the Gloucester. He seemed to believe it was urgent.

She was gone through the curtain, the folds still, unruffled. He closed the front door.

In the public bar he said: You've landed me in it, leaving a message about this place.

Harry said: Well, where else. I had to see you.

This was a hunting ground of my late uncle. Not something to be talked about in that house.

I didn't know, mate. I've got a problem and I had to see you.

The bar almost empty, before the after work regulars, the casual drinkers on their way home, or those users of the saloon bar delaying still further their nightly journey homeward from the ferry down the road. Two main bars, separated by the cubicle of the bottle department, a social register of the district, a division sharp and unaltered by time. He wrote a piece about it, but could find no ending. Starting as brief, satirical, but somehow fading. Depressing him, as the bar itself did, and he would rather have gone to another meeting place.

So the problem, he said. You've been matched with a good southpaw.

I can handle that. They set them up, I put the bastards down. Molly dookers don't worry me. No. I've got some stuff I'm short of space to store for a while. A few boxes.

I can help you move them. If that's what you want.

Not move them. Store. Store the bludgers. That house of yours.

Not mine.

There'd be room out the back. There's that shed.

My uncle's garden shed. I don't think it's ever been opened since he died.

So we could use it.

Possible, I suppose. When?

Now. I'm parked round the corner.

Heavy trees along the broken pavement of a narrow lane shielded the car. A vacant block opposite, scrub and grey sand. The back of the car stacked neatly with plain cartons under the cover Harry lifted.

Only this lot. A corner in the shed will do.

I don't know about this, he said. But it's not my house and I can't run the old girl into trouble. If there is any strife I can't front for you.

It'll be right. Just till I get the word.

His aunt said: A very peculiar young man. Very abrupt. But polite.

He's a boxer actually.

And he keeps things like that for a sideline?

Something like that.

The cartons smeared long streaks of dust in the shed. He almost forgot them. One morning his aunt said they had gone. They must have gone last night, she said.

The article was inconspicuous. Cultural Poverty. Like a headline of the depression years, grown smaller, less assertive, by now displaced by bolder type claiming a better economic world. He bought the paper on the way back to his room in the early afternoon. His aunt no subscriber to the idea of newsprint, the voices of the wireless cabinet telling her whatever she needed to know. He did not know who Hartley Grattan might have been, but the words were sudden assurance, confirmation. Plain in their statement. *Few serious studies in Australia of national development and the men who played a creative part in it. Official biographies and stuffed shirt studies valueless. No biographies of John Dunmore Lang, Barton, Fisher.* The words the tolling of a bell. *No analytical study of the role of the Labor Party in Australia.* He looked at the green leaves of the mulberry tree at the window and laughed. How could such studies have been. They were heresy. The middle ages live, he said. He held the paper near the light from the window. The words in the small type sharp. *Australia had not yet reached a size when acquaintance with literature was considered socially creditable, books no more than leisure hour distraction from the real business of living, literature a poor competitor with sport and gambling. No indigenous culture.*

Through the philosophy tutorial in the evening the printed words formed themselves with his own, dangled once oddly from Plato and his republic. Were met with uneasy glances and occasional plain incomprehension, and he knew anger, that he could not contain his words. As the room emptied he said: I'm sorry. I was confused. I've been thinking of Hartley Grattan.

I suspected, the professor said. I saw the paper. I gather you agree.

I agree, he said. Though it should not have had to wait for someone outside to say it.

In the darkness he dropped from the slowing trolley bus near the end of Mounts Bay Road, and climbed the wooden steps of Jacobs Ladder up the face of Mount Eliza, a light rain like mist, and the lights of the ferry from the darkness below him. He cut through the Observatory grounds, the side streets empty.

A bin of rubbish, small pieces of wood, narrowed the lane along the side of the house. He stood in the shadow of the verandah. Light through the thin drawn curtains. She said: I didn't expect you.

I wanted to show you something. This.

He put his books on the bed. She looked at the page of newspaper.

I'm painting.

Read it.

After. I can't let this dry.

The wide sheet of paper was pinned to the pine surface of the table, long washes of watercolour, running, the edges fusing. Starting from the beach, the dunes, greys, the stronger stain of the sea.

Another of those.

Another. Yes.

It's a new way of doing it, I suppose.

Not if you've ever seen Turner.

Have I ever seen him?

We have never seen a real Turner. Either of us.

I've never seen what I brought you to read.

In a minute, she said. These colours all seem hard and sharp, but they're very subtle. When you look.

She worked easily, quickly, confident, she had changed to the old dress she often wore when she was painting, a faded print, once, he thought, very striking. Sleeveless. A black sleeveless sweater, her full white arms, her breasts loose against the material. The water on the paper fused and ran, edging, held from the disaster he half expected by her certainty, a control she seemed to make easy. Clever, he said. But I don't think I like it.

No one likes it, she said. I do it here. Not much encouragement in class. One of the teachers said I should learn to draw. In a polite way. But that was what he meant.

Actually you can draw with a lot of skill.

Yes, she said. But that's how it is.

Like writing. Everything has to be clear. They mean obvious.

When she put the brushes away she said: I'll make some tea. Then I'll read your piece.

She set the cups and teapot on the space of table left by the paper. The pine surface held a long stain of paint.

What would happen if you ran tea over that?

I don't know, she said. I'll try it next time.

She sat beside him on the bed. She said: Did Harry take the boxes away from your aunt's shed?

Some one did.

Don't you know?

I don't want to know. They flew in the night.

Did your aunt like that?

I think it intrigued her.

I'd have thought she'd be annoyed.

She doesn't seem to get annoyed. You can't tell. Things go inside, with her. I've always felt you wouldn't want her for an enemy. I don't think she'd come up against anyone like Harry.

Who has.

He says he can find me work if I get tired of what he calls fucking about down there.

You have odd friends, she said. Would Harry let me draw him?

Read the article.

She read slowly, deliberately, a slow reader taking time to finish books he could find a way through in an hour. Then commenting on something he had missed. You have to take a chance, he said. There are too many to wait. He rested his face against her arm, his lips on the clear skin, cool, unexpectedly soft.

Don't, she said. That, or your Hartley Grattan.

Grattan, then.

She wore a plain black dress, a grey and white scarf, fine patterned. With my kind of figure, she said, black is best. Her hair, smooth, caught the light from the shop window as she turned. You could wear white. Contrast. It's not all that important, she said. But he thought she had a sudden strong beauty as she stood on the lighted pavement, waiting for him to cross the street, he touched her arm, the people about them, pushing forward to the trams, passing. She said: Will there be many there?

I don't know. The Workers Art Guild people muster a crowd at times. For someone like Grattan, I don't know.

She looked at the lighted windows, furnishing, bedroom suites, high gloss and veneer. Mirrors. Briefly they were reflected.

You should maybe join them, she said.

The Workers Art Guild?

They do get things done.

I'm not keen on groups. It's not something I can help.

No, she said. Essentially, no. Neither am I.

Near the end of the Hay Street block, where there were the car salesrooms, he stopped. In the unlighted window the machine was lean, compact, the triangular frame. Small red tank.

A Rudge, he said. It's fairly new out here.

Speedway, she said. I'll come with you one night. But you don't go often now.

I used to. Someone I knew from the country came down here to work in a garage. He built a bike and I used to watch him. He didn't finish too often. Yes, we should go.

The big room at the top of the stairs was already crowded. They sat at the back, he had not expected so many to come. Now, with the sense of surprise of the newspaper article acccpted, lessened, the words still brought recognition. Though the speaker might not know how many, or how few, how very few it was likely, had read the books he talked of with such confidence. Such easy assurance. Books hard enough to find. To order. To wait for. Some forbidden as imports to this community held about the banks of its slow river, which the speaker could know so little. The vigour of American literature and criticism came through the words, confirmation of his own reading. A reading at least of some of the fiction. He had been able to find none of the critical books. A tradition of dissent, Grattan said. Established in America. And how should that arise here. At the door, afterwards, he stopped, though she would have gone on down the stairs, and Joe Messer said:

A literature of dissent. Here.

Odd you should say that.

They wouldn't let Kisch land in the bloody place when he tried to come here. They banned Harcourt's book because it did dissent. You've got it all ahead of you, mate.

Don't look at me, he said.

The street was wet with sudden rain, glistening along the tram lines. The shop windows darkened. She said: But he's right. It is ahead of you.

Yes, he said. I'm reading Farrell and I'm trying to get Dos Passos *U.S.A* trilogy. I've never heard of Edmund Wilson. So a visitor stands up there and tells us what we should do.

I think he's right. And your friend. We didn't want Egon Kisch getting into the country. Or Mrs Freer. That had to be a joke. A dictation test in Italian. So she couldn't get in and corrupt us. And all your banned books. We do defend our shores. Yes. I think they are right.

He held her arm at the intersection, a few cars moving slowly on the wet street. In the cafe, a couple at one of the tables. Near the counter a man, alone, drinking coffee. Smoking. The cafe silent. He said: It's a kind of trap.

Being here?

Yes. And what I have to do. From here.

Going away would at least be a perspective.

You always say that, he said. Painting is different.

As you always say.

Art is a universal language, if you like. A cliche, but yes.

Writing is not?

No. And I'm not sure how that is to be worked out.

She touched his hand, her fingers still on his. Come home with me. I don't want to be by myself.

Outside, she said: That man in there.

Alan Croft.

Everyone seems to listen to his radio session.

Even my aunt. If that's a recommendation.

Sad, somehow. Sitting there. In that place. I could have drawn him. I might later.

Fame, he said. In the great city. To lift one of my family's phrases, it's no wonder he drinks.

Does he?

It does improve his session.

The rain drove across the street. She said: Why are there no trams when it rains.

In the room she took off her dress, hung it in the narrow corner wardrobe, her shoes and stockings. She stood by the table, looking down at the stained surface. He said: Don't mind me. Draw whatever it is. Is it him?

She moved the sketching block. I want to lay him to rest. He bothers me.

She worked quickly, he watched the light on her bare shoulders and arms, the sheet, the two thin blankets drawn over him on the bed. Warmth coming slowly. I could always watch you, he said. And something I was going to tell you. Grattan reminded me. A book I found. A war novel. Australian. By Leonard Mann.

Aren't you reading the wrong books?

Am I?

For someone opposed to war.

A kind of awful fascination. You may be right. It's this guilt thing I have because I feel the way I do about it.

I wonder.

Growing up on that farm. I'm not sure the place wasn't more of a battleground than I realised. I don't know if my father and my uncle tossed up for who would go to their war, but my father stayed to keep the property. They'd only just started, they would have lost it. What tensions that caused, and my uncle coming back as he did, I don't know.

You never talked about it with your father?

Strictly something we never talked about. But I resent I should have any sort of guilt. If I do.

So where does the book come in?

It's a good description of what I suppose that shambles was like. But right at the end, he comes up with the nation established on the battle field idea, then he suggests, very quietly as if it might be blasted away, the other idea that out of it all there might also be the birth of what he calls a small creative ferment. And he says only by science, letters, and art can a people become great. He hopes for a new flowering, presumably of these things.

The flowering wasn't very obvious.

I admire him for saying it. But it comes after all the words, the wreckage, the nation founded on slaughter idea. I've never been able to see why that is where a nation is born. It's obscene.

Very. Was it a good book?

I think it was. It was honest.

She held up the block. This is how it has to be. I can work it from here.

Yes, he said. Haunting. Sad enough. I think you frighten me.

Strange seeing him like that. It fitted my mood.

I think I'll go home.

No you won't. And you can give me the warm side. It's cold out there.

This bed hasn't got two sides.

She lay against him. Still. Her hands and arms cold. She said: If you meet me after work Saturday. For lunch. I'll have something for you to carry.

You haven't bought a painting? No. You wouldn't do that.

The room dark. Quiet. Someone moving in the passage. She said: I hope the old bat is not hanging about out there.

She unwrapped the heavy parcel. I saw this in the

bookshop window. I couldn't get it until today. I had to draw the money out.

The book lay, solid, on the brown paper. The Botticelli head and thick gold tresses holding the centre of the cover. *A Treasury Of Art Masterpieces.* Thomas Craven. The legend simple. Clear. She said: I had to have it. I'm almost afraid to open it. It might not be there.

It will be there. It has a fine solidity. I carried it.

They sat at the table and she opened the heavy cover carefully. The light lessened in the room, the afternoon drawing to cloud, and once they heard the rain. I never knew there were these paintings, she said. Not that they were. And not like this.

She got up from the table. I'm sorry. The lunch got missed. I'll find us something.

He moved the book for her to set the plates on the table. Leave the drawings at the end, she said. They're finished. For now. Perhaps for ever after seeing that book.

No, he said. It's not like that.

I have to see these paintings. I have to. I don't believe them.

Something like El Greco's *Toledo In A Storm*, yes. I didn't know anything had that power.

All our lives we've never known it existed. You go to the Gallery and it's those same things. All day. Every day. How can anyone ever know about these paintings.

The American work, he said. Burchfield. His *November Evening.* That sombre building. A kind of grey-brown. The clouds. The horses coming round that curve. All the light going.

A terrible emptiness. The man is the same as the land.

It has the same power as American writing.

She said: You see why I have to go. Don't you.

I see there is nothing here. How could there be. I mean, these paintings.

We should go out for a while.

It's raining.

It's stopped, she said. I just want to walk.

The heavy clouds held above the line of hills, the buildings of the city dark, the river still. Perth in a storm, he said.

They walked slowly. He said: Something I was going to tell you. The book made me forget, but it's the same thing. There's a new tutor, from Melbourne. He has a very striking portrait someone did of him over there. Different. Very strong. Like some of the things you do. Striking, rather hard colours, angles.

Could I see it?

I think so. But it was something he said. I was asking him how he found things here. That sort of idiot thing. And he said I suppose what I find most obvious here is a lack of passion. It startled me. I mean, no one talks like that.

A very subversive comment. He'll have to be careful.

He won't stay.

In the room she said: I suppose we should have a proper meal. It's late.

He touched her shoulders, turning her, and she said: Well, later. As she lay on the bed he stood looking down at her. He began to laugh.

Why am I funny?

You're one of those paintings. Renaissance. Plush. Spread. The goddess. Though they don't have your dark hair. Not in the reproductions.

Not the little Cranach goddess.

Not a Cranach girl at all.

Perhaps you shouldn't do this, she said. There must be a penalty for loving goddesses.

She worked carefully, small pieces of colour, trying to mix, to work the paint on the smooth board she held, like dough, like making bread. Like his mother. Once. The bread set in big tubs on the hearth, covered, overnight. Small cakes she made when neighbours were coming. Gatherings at the wide table on the verandah. Talk he had not understood. On three smaller canvases she had worked parts of the old outcamp. Two of them long sweeps of the boards of the verandah, veined and knotted, rich streaks of colour, an ochre, lemon coloured knots, whorls of darker browns, greys that lay in swathes, lightening to white, or edged to umber. The third held two of the galvanised iron sheets, twisted, rich with the encrustation of rust, streaks of silver, hard brown grooves. Now she worked slowly on a bigger canvas, propped on the table against the wall. She stretched forward, her arms bare, the thin dress drawing about her shoulders, across her hips. I like canvas, she said. I know it costs more. I can buy it while I'm working. It's traditional, he said. That's why you like it. I'm not traditional, she said. And you wouldn't know. The outcamp against a flat landscape, land without feature, grey, but with faint suggestions of colour, as if some life lay there still. The house barely distinguished from it, without the richness of the smaller paintings, long ago absorbed in that landscape. Given to it. She said: Do you think I'm getting tangled with your Burchfield?

No, he said. It seems to stand away from that. Colour. Your long washes of colour. Even when nearly all the colour's gone. Rather than detail. But what you have is true. It would disturb my parents. If they understood it. If I understand it.

I'd give it to them if they liked it.

They were very proud of their new house. Well, so was I. Perhaps they've forgotten that one. No, I don't think you should give it to them.

Does it disturb you?

It disturbs me that you can put down like that what I have to struggle for.

We're back on our old theme, she said.

You've worked all the morning. We could take lunch down to the University. Then go to the art lecture.

You get it, she said. While I have a shower. But do you like it?

Yes. It's very good. But the thing is, you don't care, I mean it doesn't matter, does it, if I like it or not.

No, she said. How could it.

On the south side of the Hall there was shade from the heavy clump of trees. A kind of jungle, she said, holding out against all this knowledge. She looked at the patches of grass, and he spread his handkerchief on the broken turf. Not that you'll get much of it on that, he said.

It will save some of the grass stains. She looked up at the tower that lifted above the Hall, sharp against the hard clear sky. Can you go up there?

Ted Wright and I have lunch up there some days. He's worried about Kant. He says it gives him a better perspective up there.

Would you take me?

It's a long climb. I don't know if it's open on Sundays.

A week day. When I have time. I want to paint from there. A kind of Monet thing. Looking out over there to the Park and the river.

Do you think you should do a Monet thing? Deliberately, as an influence?

Not as an influence. No. I want to understand what I think those painters were doing. I've never seen a real Monet.

Who has. If you stare at the tower, it's falling. Against the sky.

From where you are. Most of you lying all over my lap.

That's a curious word. But you do have one. Try looking at the tower.

When you leave here, she said. What then? Writing is no living.

I need to read. I like the university. But I can get only a vague idea how much there is to read. The library, that little bit at the end of the building, through the arch. Almost nothing Australian. I want to do a thesis on Australian writing. There aren't the books. Not even the books on Australian history I'd need as well. It wouldn't be much different anywhere else. No Australian university has a chair in Australian history. Grattan was right. A lot of the books haven't been written yet.

So painting is easier. Well it's not. But you still have to find something when you finish. Teaching?

I'd like never to finish. I suppose the idea would be something like a tutor here. But how would I ever get that.

When you have a degree?

They don't believe in their own degrees. You have to jump through the right hoops. Go abroad. Oxford or Cambridge. A fake conditioning. Then you come back and are respectful. It's this England thing all the time. A degree here might be a bit thin. Very thin in some respects. But the answer is not to chase off to England. They don't know we exist.

You could study there.

It has no relevance.

Research.

They wouldn't have heard of what I want to research.

You could come with me and try it out.

It's time for the art lecture. You can ask awkward questions there. Though the lecturer does seem to have answers.

Of course, she said. He's been to England.

The downstairs bar was quiet, two drinkers in one of the corners, a barmaid polishing glasses, her hair bright against the mirror behind her. Harry said: If I ever retire

I'll live down here. But what I'm saying, this is just a favour. Small stuff. Out to the Sterling Arms. North Perth. You go in the back, off the back street. Ask for George.

What happens if someone wants to know what I'm doing?

No bastard's going to ask that. Leave the car in the street behind my place after. I'll be in there about five. Take you back to town.

The small back yard of the hotel was empty. Rubbish piled by bins against the fence. Cases of empty bottles. Amber in the late sun. Quiet. He took the cartons into the small dark store room. The smell of cooking, the bars deserted. The man offered him a drink. In the streets there was little traffic and he drove slowly. Driving here was different from the only other driving he did, the wheat carting, his father's truck along the roads of summer, the dust and the heat, the clatter of the elevator at the bins. He had tried to form a story from the small transactions, the missions he undertook for Harry, but could find no climax, no resolution. Just a thing done. It goes on, Harry said. No harm. People need things. He left the car in the street, in Fremantle, small houses, white painted, set close to the road, some with yards at the back where fishing nets dried. He sat on the verandah of the house that was almost on the footpath, and where there was no sound from inside, but where others slept. A kind of lodging house, owned it seemed by a relative of Harry. Harry did not offer, or seek some kinds of information. He came down the road, walking quickly, opened and closed the white gate with an odd care, taking the parcels he carried into a small room at the front. Better deliver you, he said. The factory?

Too late now. The ferry will do. I can get a bus from here if you're pushed.

I've got to go through to Vic Park. I'll drop you.

His driving had a careless confidence, deceptive, like his

boxing. He said: Pay you Friday. Okay? You wouldn't want to make a run Sunday?

Sunday?

I'm working. Have to be an early run.

But what does he want you to do? Barbara said.

Just deliver.

Deliver what?

I don't ask. And Harry gets his own orders.

You mean it's all right as long as you don't know.

I don't mean anything.

It's crazy.

You could see Harry that way. But then another way he makes a lot of sense.

He stopped the van outside the house in Colin Street and went down the side. She said: I'm ready. You can carry these.

You're going to like the vehicle.

At the gate she said: This? You didn't say it was a van.

I didn't know. Room for your painting gear.

Is it full? No, don't tell me. You don't know.

I doubt it. But I'd rather drive one of these than a car.

I don't think I like this.

I told you I don't ask what Harry does. A lot of it's probably quite reasonably legitimate.

Like what?

I don't know. Ways round tax. Duties. Agency agreements.

Nothing would be stolen.

I don't know.

Just drive.

Beyond the Midland Town Hall, a few streets east, he turned left. He said: At least we're on time.

What will they say when they see me?

What would anyone say.

Where the houses ended he turned down a track to an isolated house and sheds. Two men came towards them.

He backed the van close to a larger carrier's van, handed one of the men the key.

Barbara said: Don't you do anything?

I drive. This lot's going on further, I'd say. End of the road for us.

No, she said. We're going up into the hills. For the day. If you remember.

The road climbed steeply to the edge of the scarp, a road narrow and broken and she said: I hope this van runs backwards. They walked from where the road ended, along the railway that followed the edge of the slope. Below them the line lay in zig zag sweeps down the face of the scarp. Like lines of trenches, he said. Those drawings you used to see of the trenches in France.

I don't think I ever did see any, she said.

When I was a child. My family seemed to have magazines full of war pictures.

She drew the long spears of the blackboys that were greening, the small helmet shaped buds roughening their surface. Sitting on the long slope of rock he watched her, the spears standing against the clear light sky. They are very old, he said. Things from a dead landscape.

Morbid, she said. Eat your lunch.

I've been reading *Death Of A Hero*. I got it at last. They must have lifted the ban. Or forgotten. I fell asleep over it last night.

Exciting. She picked up the sandwich from the smooth rock. Your aunt is better at lunches than I am.

There's an ant on it.

She held out the bread. Move it.

He let the brown thick body move along his hand. It's interesting in the problem he had to get it published as he wanted. Bits of it are still censored. Neat asterisks. And his introduction is quite bitter. About trying to force some freedom into writing. Though there are bits I'm not sure I follow. But the war scenes have a terrible sense of final destruction. There's a passage sticks in my mind. I don't think I'll ever forget it. Winterbourne, the captain, has almost reached the end, he's looking at the battle field, the whole ghastly lunacy of what is left, and there's a beautiful sentence that ends something like, he stood in frozen silence and contemplated the last achievements of civilised men.

Below, across the grey plain there were the small blocks of the city, the expanse of the river, hazed, distant. She said: Can I read it?

Of course. And of course they weren't the last achievements.

Civilised men are very persistent.

Indeed. Those places stink of death. I don't know why you want to go there. They've never solved anything except by war.

I was afraid we'd get to that. What would you have? Now. The way things are?

Neutrality, he said. A proud neutrality, if you like.

You won't get much support for that sort of innovation here.

I know that. This is all bigger and better Gallipolies.

Strange how that has stuck.

There is a kind of counter current. Almost a counter culture. Very faint. They will kill it.

She held out the sketch block. What do you think?

The clear sharp spears of the blackboys twisted away from the green bushes, the dark trunks, the spiked spare leaves of undergrowth, where there were a few reddish-orange flowers.

You've made it very powerful. Very strong.

It's harsh, she said. All this. It will have to be black and white.

Below the rocks the seaweed was dry and brittle. Waves cut slowly at the base of the brown weed, long thin spines holding in the sand, flexing, the weed stripped from them. Like a miniature dead forest, he said. Invaded by the sea. A new land forming.

The weed is like a land mass, she said. A diagram in a text book. Something from your *Science Of Life*. Do you think Wells saw something like this?

I doubt he spent a lot of time at the seaside. I waited all my life for that book. I wish it had been there when I was at school.

Would you have understood it?

No. But neither would many of my teachers. And they certainly wouldn't have used it.

Too many books lately, she said. I don't keep up.

It's freeing, somehow. I don't know, luck perhaps. Or they are forcing their way in here. The war could put it all back again.

What do you think happens to all those little flying things when the weed goes?

Lay eggs somewhere and with a bit of patience it all goes on again.

Patience, she said. God. I'm fed up waiting.

The sun had little warmth, the light sharp. A thin bank of cloud held to the north, beyond the point, darkening over the land. He said: What do your parents think of you going away?

They don't understand at all. But they never have. When I was at school it was great that I was good at art. A nice thing for a girl to do. When they saw I was serious about it, that was different. Women were not professional painters. I think they had a horrible idea they were going to have to support me for life.

Would they have?

No. I couldn't go quickly enough for them. Out of the house. That place was all they cared about. No, they were never interested in me. Now they think this is some strange thing, like an illness. Or that it's because of you.

They did meet me once. Are you sure it's not?
You are my lover.
There will be others.
I don't know.

With her bare foot she smoothed the patch of sand where she had been tracing with a thin piece of rush. She marked firmly on the sand an intricate pattern that he saw was forming a monogram of her initials linked with his own. He said: You went with Ray Sands before I met you.

Ray and I grew up in the same street. It was something bound to happen sometime. It was no great thing. No, she said. It's you. And more than that. You are my friend.

Yes. And I don't see why we have to lose that.
It won't be lost.
I don't understand how you say that.
You understand. And I'll write to you. I'll probably come back. You may change your mind and come over there.
If there's anything left of the place to come to.
That makes me feel a lot better. Thanks.
No. I'm sorry, he said. I just don't know what I'm going to do. Here.

The bar was crowded. Harry said: Wait till this stuff gets rationed.
You think it will?
It's what they say. Have to be.
That could cause a certain amount of civil unrest.
There'll be some money in it.
He watched the two women behind the bar. Will you be in that?
It'll be there. Why not. But it will be hard. You going to register?

I'll have to, he said.

Once you're on that they've got you.

If I want to finish at the university I'll have to. They'll ask questions.

They can't ask questions if you're not on it.

I'm enrolled at the university. They don't have to be that bright.

They're not bright. And it'll be something you can buy.

I'd hardly risk that, he said. Even if I had the money. And it was possible.

It'll be bad. Identity cards. The lot. Conscription for anywhere. I know a few won't register.

You?

I don't know, Harry said. I can get on the wharves now.

You're joking.

No. If I want it. The uncle can get it through.

I don't believe this.

They know I'm safe, mate.

And you will?

I'm not sure. They could start taking a few from down there. I'd be registered. No different from your bloody university. Up shit creek.

You're more certain about all this than I am.

I've battled. I don't owe the bastards anything. If I could get over east I'd go. Sydney or Melbourne. Melbourne, I'd say. It's too hard here. Too small. Every bastard knows every other bastard. There's a chance I could go.

I think I'll see how it works out, he said. Just go with it. For a while.

From the gym they turned down past the Central Police Station by the corner of Roe Street, the doorway lit, the light hardly breaking the shadow of the pavement. Harry said: If you're not coming, I'll see you later, walking fast, flexing his shoulders and arms, stepping left, forward, an old fighter's shuffle, seeing himself, the footwork. Ernie

Blake and his gymnasium. Living his old fights. But fast and good in his day. It could happen like that. It might. The small houses were lit, curtains over the doors and windows, light behind the latticed verandahs. Opposite, a long row of railway carriages. An engine shunting somewhere beyond the bridge. Near the end of the line of houses, by the street that lifted to the curving bridge across the railway, holding little traffic, a tram moving at the curve, he turned in, jumped the low steps where in the hot afternoons the women sat, showing their legs, open thighs. There were no men in the front room. In the back, a room once a kitchen, a wood stove he had never seen used, a tea pot, tea things on its clean dark plates. One of the girls said: Harry. You're early. Can't wait, he said. She laughed, touched the bottle on the table. He said: Not now, Jenny. Where's Rose?

The girl lifted her hand towards the side door. You're early for Rose. And French isn't here yet. She's late. But she was here this afternoon.

Rose I want, he said. He knocked on the door. A woman said: Go a bloody way dear.

Business, Rose, he said.

The room was dark. From the bed Rose said: I'm tired. Whatever it is, no, Harry.

You haven't heard, he said. There's no problem.

In the front room French said: Surprise. I've just got here. You're early.

We're going out.

I'm working.

Not tonight. He turned her back towards the door. Briefly her thin bare arm held him.

You'll have to see Rose.

Rose is nicely pissed. I've seen her. It's okay.

She said: Have you waited long. You haven't been with Jenny?

Don't be bloody silly.

As they crossed the verandah she said: There might be trouble.

No. I've had a good week. It's fixed.

One day they'll bloody fix you Harry.

In the car he thought she was asleep, but crossing the bridge into the port she looked at the boats in the harbour, lifting her hand to her hair as if against the wind.

You working on any of those?

Too busy, he said. He parked the car near the small cafe, the pavement dark, the light inside dimmed. The cafe was empty.

Life, she said. You got to come down here to see it.

He went to a table in the middle of the room, she walked slowly, as tall as he was, thin, with dark short hair, her face thin, sharp. Steak, Tony, he said. Everything. The lot. She ate as much as he did, never gaining weight. You've got a bloody worm, French, he said. It's how I get a living, she said. Not that some are that long.

I might have to go away, he said.

You mean you are.

Something like that. Over east. Melbourne.

You've talked about it, she said.

If I don't go now it could be too hard to get out of here. The bastards will close it up.

If you have to.

There's going to be nothing here. Too small. Every bugger running round with a dog tag. Those that are left. Over there it's going to be big. People will want things.

They want things here.

They're not going to get them.

She touched her mouth with a handkerchief, her movements quick, strong, unexpected, a journalist who went to Rose's, and had covered some of his fights, a few lines after the main bout report, saying Rene has a talent for writhing. It's an art form. I'm going to do a piece about it and leave it in my editor's out tray. It can go in the *Mail*.

On the Red Page.
Don't pick your nose, he said. Listen. I can get work over there. Reserved occupation. I'll send for you.
And you'll be working at that?
Not working at that. It'll be set up. Someone with defence contracts. But that's not what I'll be doing.
They're closing down on the black over here.
It never got started over here. I'll fix it for you to come.
I'm not working in any bloody defence factories. Or rag sweat shops. No. I won't go, Harry.
You won't have to work.
You making me an honest woman?
How would I do that. But they're not going to like you leaving. French, don't pick your bloody nose.
It itches.
Leave it. I'll most likely get someone on a boat to tell you. They're opening bloody letters, there's some little shit high Hitlers in the censorship and the manpower. I won't write. But you'll have to do what he says. And just go.
I'm not that proud, she said. Okay. Can I have an icecream? To finish.
Tony saw you coming. He'll have it lined up.
In the street she said: This place has died.
There'll be a boat in the weekend.
You sure?
Full of your favourite fighting men.
I need the money.
If I get you to Melbourne you won't need to worry.
Great.
You're not going back there tonight. You can come round to my place.
She said: I don't know which is bloody worse.

In the quiet of the library the books were painted on the walls. A set. Characters moving to the foot of the narrow stairs. Words for the narrow walkways above. Juliet waiting. A long wait here. Where no one spoke. In the late winter cold. Where indeed not many came. His notes in the folder. He said: A dead end. Janet. Would you like a coffee?

She closed her book, a slip of paper in the place.

Yes. It's cold in here.

An unlikely tomb.

Oh really. But you do look depressed.

Your psychologists would have a name for it.

They might. But it could be simpler.

The tables of the refectory were clear, most unoccupied, a group by the window, talking, beyond the glass the forecourt shadowed, clouds above the buildings. Somedays, she said, there's no one here. Other days you can't get in.

And is there a name for that?

If that's how you are, she said, I'm not staying.

I'm sorry.

You've been scratching about with those notes all the morning. You're not getting anywhere are you.

If it's so obvious. No. Nowhere.

If your thesis is not what you want to do, why do you go on with it?

You ask all the right questions, Janet. I don't know the answers.

At least the coffee is hot, she said. Of course you do.

Not the right answers. The simple answer is that for the thesis I want to do I'd have to go to the Mitchell Library. There are no books here.

Your Australian thing. It would be a problem.

An impossibility.

You could do it after the war.

It's now I'm worried about. I want to do this now. I think it has to be done. It's important.

Well, so is the war, I suppose.

At the table by the window one of the men was standing, gesticulating. The others laughing.

There was a sense of nationalism, he said. A kind of realisation of this country, an awareness, coming out of the last few years. And now it's all going to find expression in war.

Is that bad? I mean, the way things are.

It won't find expression in writing. Art. Discussion. It'll be conveniently buried in war. A perfect bloody irony.

She was looking at the cup on the table, her fingers turning it in a small arc. Left. To the right. Her oval face carefully made up, a white mask, deep red lips, a film star copy, he had always wanted to say that. Her brown hair waved, held. Not vain, but aware and pleased she was noticed. They had started in the same year, shared some classes, talked, an edge, a dislike between them, he was not sure what it should be called. She did not look up, her fingers touching the cup. She said:

Those things have to wait, surely.

The official view, yes.

Is there another?

You ask odd questions. For a psychologist.

You're not trying to say the individuality thing. Everyone the right to their own choice.

Perhaps I'd prefer some kind of belief in trying to understand. Understand history. Writing.

This is history.

And a belief in rationalism, he said. Not this kind of cultivated sentimentality that is everywhere now. Whatever you call it. Whatever flag you fly it from.

So what will you do?

I don't know.

Some people will be afraid to go.

Some will be afraid to stay.

There may be no choice.

Our masters will see to that. If you finish your degree you may be able to work on a few of the returning examples. Last time it was much simpler. They shot the shock cases.

He saw the careful mask of her face. Don't worry, he said. We have our separate fates, Janet. In a few weeks you will get your pass in psychology. I will hand in a thesis on a safe novelist. He put down the cup. The group by the window was breaking up. Chairs scraping. We will both leave here. Keep well.

The balcony of the Great Hall seemed deserted. He could not remember the words. And from the Hall the music. The sacrificial abandon of body and mind to rhythms as old as time. If that was how it had been written. The Hall burning with heatless fire against the black sky behind its square clock-tower. The darkness of the half invisible garden below. No name mattered to its beauty. There was no quarrel with those words, however recalled, though he would not have chosen them. He leaned against the waist high stone work, cold to his hands. Like shadow the long coat and dress. The coat held across her shoulders. The two quick steps, twisting, then forward, her body supple, balanced, the coat lifting, a cape. Then still. She said: I didn't see you.

The lights reflections in the still pool below. He said: I'm sorry to startle you, Janet.

She moved to touch the balcony, looking down, the long reflections in the water. I didn't expect to see you at something like this.

No.

I don't think I ever have.

I've been reading Mackenzie's book. The first part has a very rich description of a dance in the Hall. I thought I'd

see how it fitted. If anything had changed.
And has it? Or should I say does it?
It does fit.
I haven't seen the book.
It's ruffled a few people. He doesn't seem to care. He uses real people. Himself. Friends.
Resolving old conflicts.
Perhaps. In a place this size I'd say it was dangerous. He had to leave it.
Because of that?
Probably more that it was too small for him.
Does that worry you?
I don't think so. It might even be an advantage.
It is not an advantage, she said. Her hands lifted to the collar of the coat, drawing it about her shoulders. Her throat was bare, a single fine necklace, a small locket. She said: Well?
Nothing, he said.
I'm sorry I was on edge the other afternoon. If I was unpleasant.
No. It's a time for being on edge.
Yes it is. And you don't feel like your writer whom I've never read that this place is too small?
I don't think so. You can see more clearly. Mackenzie did.
When I came out on the balcony, she said. Did you wonder what I was doing?
I thought you were dancing.
Quite stupid. Of me. Not you. I'll tell you something. I wanted to be a dancer.
It's not something I'm any authority on.
I thought of being like Ginger Rogers. Me, and a few others, I suppose.
Janet, that is very romantic. Mackenzie might have approved of that. At least for his night piece.
I won dancing prizes when I was at school. I was in love

with those films. I am. Dancing says everything. Not messed about with words.

For a psychologist surely that's dangerous ground.

I don't think so. And how would I be a psychologist. I'm a woman. Where would I get a job like that. No. I'll be a teacher.

Psychology seems a fairly rare profession anyhow. Are there any in Perth?

What does it matter. She said: I came to this dance with John and Mary and a few others. I've lost them.

I'm sorry.

Actually they're drinking. At the cars. Her hand lifted, moving at the darkness. Over there.

Where you were.

Where I was. How do you know?

A sort of perfume of evidence.

Fine. Would you dance with me?

I'm very inadequate. If you're looking for an Astaire.

No, she said. Just dancing will do.

They moved among the moving bodies. For ever advancing upon the backward-bent body for ever retreating. Desire unspoken. Had they been the words? Amongst these. With desires more easily satisfied. He said: Is it like your films?

No, she said. The films are America.

America is *The Grapes Of Wrath*.

If that is another book, she said. I haven't read it.

Why did you choose psychology?

It worked out that way. I thought there might be room for teaching in psychology. The war will stop that.

It will stop everything. Except our real preoccupation.

Thank you for dancing, she said. I think the others have come back.

The dead trees were dark against the salt, the gimlets a thin shade along the edge of the white ground, their trunks clear, shining in the last of the light. He drew the truck to the side of the road, and walked to the edge of the trees. By the patches of samphire the birds stepped slowly. There was little water, the salt barely crusted. In parts broken.

At the table, in the lighted room, he said: There were avocets along the salt pan. A bit late for them.

They stay at times, his father said. There's still water in the lakes.

The salt is spreading.

No. I don't think so.

The trees are all dead in the south corner.

His father did not speak. The evenings were the worst. In the day, carting from the harvester, driving to the bins, the hard clear light, the heat, the trees along the roadside and the shifting lines of shade made a pattern they did not question. At night, in the wide room that seemed never quite lit by the two lamps, they could not escape one another. His mother said: Will you stay for the seeding?

That's a time yet. It's not likely to be my decision.

You have finished your exams.

Yes. Three years, and I begin to understand some things. Not well, but a beginning.

It is what you wanted.

Yes. And now I'm likely to be forced into a total mindlessness. Where none of those things matter.

You won't have much use for your degree or your mind if this country is taken over by enemies.

Her face lined, emphasised in the lamp light. Taut. He said: I'm not sure how different that would be. This place has never exactly had any use for the artist.

Do you call yourself that?

Artist? A way of speaking, he said. Forget it.

His father said: I could put in to the manpower to have you here.

I doubt they'd listen.

But that wouldn't be what you want. Not now.

I'm not sure it ever was.

Once. It might have been. But we have never stood in your way.

I know that. I know that and I'm grateful.

Your father could try, his mother said.

They wouldn't listen. They're stripping the country. This State will have the highest percentage of people in the services of any in Australia. The little men in the manpower have to justify themselves somehow.

That is quite stupid.

And I can't do that. It would be a wrong decision. No decision at all.

At least it would be useful, his mother said. You could apply for exemption as a conscientious objector if you really are so much against war.

Are you serious?

Though that would not be very well thought of about here.

And that worries you.

Why shouldn't it? We have been here all our lives.

There is no need for this, his father said.

Conscientious objection, he said. You can see what the magistrates do with them. They're not about to open that gate. You'd have to be an ordained preacher. The idea of conscientious objection has never been admitted here. The magistrates know what is expected. No. I wouldn't claim that. I don't say I'm that.

I'm sure I don't know what you are, his mother said. Or why you are simply against things all the time.

No. I am for things.

For them?

Things we haven't got yet.

It might be better if we never do. And what happened to your friend? Barbara.

She went to England. I told you.

That was brave of her.

She had her own beliefs.

Outside, in the darkness, he walked to the gates of the far paddock, by the roadway, felt the cold bars that once as a child he had painted. The paint flaked now, the metal with the spread of rust. His father smiling. If you want to do it. You can paint the house when you have done that. He had been proud of the bright shining gates as they approached from the road. Rust near the heavy bolt and chain, a roughness beneath his hand. The words of the house lost in the darkness and the silence. He ran his hand along the cold frame. Old father, old artificer, stand me now and ever in good stead. Fly close to the sun, Icarus. The words selfconscious, but as if he knew them for the first time. But not this sun. But yes. Yes. This sun. The small figure plunging to the sea beside the boat, its sails filled, on the land the horse and plough turning the long curve of neat flat furrows. The goats browsing among the rocks. They are sheep, Barbara said. I will leave the book with you. No, he said, you will need it. No. I will see them. Brueghel and all the others. But he would not take the book. In the darkness the gate moved in a small arc under his hand.

The two men behind the counter turned sheets of paper. At times staring at the counter, looking towards the door, shielded from the street. As if they no more believed in all this than he did. No one else in the small office. Outside, the street dark. The air warm. Clear. One of the men touched a piece of paper. Another hour. Now they did not know. An airways office. It would not rate a second class rail terminal. Just say Harry will meet her, he said. Okay? He walked slowly down the street, the buildings darkened, a group of Americans, no women. Later the M.Ps, the waggons on the street, there were some now. He walked the block, past the central railway station, back, edging through the angled doorway that held the light from the street. She was standing by the counter.

French, he said.

She turned slowly. A thin black coat. Dark dress that took the light. Her face white. Tired.

I've been waiting, he said. I just went out.

It could have been the wrong place, she said. I wouldn't know.

No one would say when the bloody plane was due.

That thing. How would they know.

The plane was the only chance. How was it?

Alright when it was up. Bumpy. But it kept coming down. I didn't know there were that many places it could land.

He said: That your bag? It's fairly light.

Not that much to put in it.

We'll have to get the train. We could just make the last one. Midnight. I couldn't bring a car. Problems at this time of night.

You've got a car.

I drive one.

I've never been over here.

Me neither. It's a big city. Quite a lot of it. You'll find your way round.

You could drive me.

They might not like that.

God who is it this time?

Let's catch the train, he said. There are better places than around here at this time. And taxis cost money.

There are taxis?

There is everything. Here.

She said suddenly: You're scared, Harry.

No, he said. Not scared. Careful.

She said: This thing is different.

Different. It's electric.

The wonders of Melbourne.

Don't knock it.

It has to be better than that plane.

She could see only darkness, the reflection of the carriage in the glass. She closed her eyes. She said: Do you think this happened?

They walked out of the empty suburban station and he said: Two blocks.

The small houses on the edge of the pavement. Close. Some had to be empty. Everyone gone from them. Long ago. Yet she did not think so. We got better in Roe Street, she said. He turned down a long row of terraces, small strips of empty ground in the front of some of the houses, a few weeds, or flowers, no colour in the darkness. Shapes, as if someone had forgotten them. Much better, she said. He turned suddenly, opened a front door, and she laughed. How do you know which one? Count, he said.

At the top of the stairs he opened a door into a single room. A bed near the window, a chest of drawers, marble topped washstand with a jug and basin. Deep blue flowers patterned on the crazed china. A wardrobe in one corner by the door. A chair. He moved the curtain and looked down into the street. It's a room, he said. But this view is useful. She stood beside him. The houses were dark.

Does anyone live here?

Plenty.

There's a cat, she said. By that window.

The loo is out the back. No bath. If you're caught short use the basin. Cold nights it's easier.

Like a hotel.

It's hard to find anywhere. I'm looking. I wasn't sure if you could get away. I'll find somewhere bigger.

You weren't sure I'd come.

That. Yes.

It would have been hard, she said. But it was all a bit quick for them. I'll give you that. You do fix things.

There's just one thing. Be careful for a while. Don't go sitting about in the pubs. Till you're settled. The vice boys will pick you up. They're big on women. The bastards. They can come expensive.

Seems like there'll be problems. She lifted her arms suddenly. When wasn't there. I'm tired. And I'm still going up and down from that plane. She drew the dark dress over her head, she had a slip and panties. The light from the window reflected her thin white body.

You're thinner, he said.

No one's been feeding me.

He held her above her hips, lifted her easily, set her down. Otherwise okay. No change.

She held him, strong, hard, her thin arms. Thanks for all this. I didn't think I'd hear from you again.

I don't know if you will ever get this letter. Or where you are. The address you gave me may no longer exist, of course. Your brief ps, that you were going to France, did you go? There has been only that one note you sent soon after you arrived. But I have to write to you. As you may have expected, the machine finally engulfed me. I seem to have given in easily, and I can only feel that was wrong. I'm not sure how it has happened, or it may be that I do not want to know. I need to talk to you. You were a kind of catalyst for me, I think. Wrong word? Leave it. I spent a period of compulsory insanity doing things I would not in fact have expected to find in an asylum. A regulated insanity. I suppose I could say before that I spent some time at the farm helping straighten things up and doing some seasonal work. I felt very strongly the kind of force the land has, and that I had to resist. A kind of trap. I went out to the old house one day but you were so strongly with me that I literally fled. However, the insanity I referred to has taken a different form and resulted in motion. Eastward. From the plain to the desert. The Nullarbor despite all I had read, all we had read, those books, and the *Walkabouts*, you said you could make a grey-white wash of it, despite everything it frightened me. I think it was fear. No one could make anything of that plain. I had a

terrible sense we travelled across the Australia that
will be when we have finished our work.
Destroying the land. Killing one another. A shift in
time and there it was. It all depresses me vastly and
I can't write happy patriotic all will be well letters.
But the red dunes and the sheoaks were something
quite different, and I thought of Finlayson's book,
and Madigan, that you gave me. I wondered what
would happen if I got off the train, a weird
concoction of freight trucks, or vans I suppose, and
carriages, all full of men, and wandered away into
this red country. It is what I should have been able
to do. To live with it. That it was impossible, for
every reason, seems to me a final tragedy. Near
evening we stopped for a meal, and unexpectedly
there were the aborigines, come down to the train,
the men, and their women and children. From
somewhere out of that place I could not exist in. I
hadn't thought a great deal about them, as you
know, until not long ago we read the articles in
Walkabout. And after you had gone I found Elkin's
book. There were some of them about the farm
when I was a child, I think I was in a way afraid of
them. But they moved away and the only places I
ever saw them was around some of the towns. This,
at the edge of the desert, was quite different. They
wore the cast off clothes of white people, ugly,
degrading. Like I remembered. But this could not
kill the grace of their movement, the quick
alertness, sudden free gesture like nothing that had
anything to do with us. Nor the fine faces of the
older men. You could only be aware of a
sensitiveness to natural things that I doubt we have
ever had. And which I have to admit I could not
remember in those I had seen about the country
towns. And they came to the train to sell articles,

take scraps of our meal. To be cheated and laughed at by creatures I've found it harder and harder to conceal contempt for. Who threw crusts and bits of food as if they would be contaminated by the touch of these people. They, dispossessed I suppose, gathering the scraps, sharing them, and each had something. We, herded in our trucks and carriages and without freedom and without dignity. Our arrogant voices breaking the silence of the red dunes and the deep-coloured sheoaks. I am haunted by it.

Melbourne is a different world. A reasonably obvious statement. I'm sorry. But a first impression indeed most obvious. There is everything here, the shops have goods, window displays, you can buy chocolates anywhere, luxuries, displays of clothes, suitcases — which so baffled you before you left — there are buses, taxis, new, quite unlike the relics we are used to — everything our poor little hairshirt community on the other side of the desert has deprived itself of so sanctimoniously. A great deal more, I suspect, if you know where to look. Something Harry finds of interest. I have met him here, he has offered one or two things of interest. I don't know, I may take him up on them. There are books here I never thought of. Second hand bookshops where I could spend all day, early Australian books beyond imagining. We never had second hand bookshops. There were few enough books. But here, Sewards in Bourke Street, Halls, other shops at the top of Bourke Street, a very interesting shop in Prahran, a man called Quayne, he has been very helpful though I am plainly a beginner and with nothing much to spend. In Sewards there are stairs that turn up into a kind of half floor and you walk up into these books. Sorry, it turns me poetic. I would buy them all. One learned proprietor who wouldn't see you if you were not wearing the right clothes, and where if you ask for a book you will be snubbed with style. New books. I bought Eliot's poems, you remember we heard that beautiful reading on the radio, Ash Wednesday. Sound gave those words meaning. I have been reading it, in an inadequate way, because its meaning beyond sound is elusive I'm afraid. And the *Hollow Men*. I have stood on parade grounds and recited those words to myself. Not altogether understanding, yet if you feel as much for them as I do that must be some measure of understanding. It did occur to me that if I suddenly orated them I might be granted a discharge on the grounds of insanity. But most likely they would simply conclude I had uttered an obscenity. You should be here, not in some part of a world that is half destroyed. And from which I don't see that much can come again. Though some painters here say they would probably go to Europe. When the war is over. If it ever is. I don't see what they hope to find there.

   This is a beautiful city. The buildings. The change of light. The way the land runs, perspectives. Looking down Bourke Street in the early morning, traffic in the mist. Collins Street in midday, the trees, sun on the fine facades. I don't know what lies behind them. Spreading endlessly, it seems, from its centre. To be discovered. You may feel like that where you are. And where you, like myself, must be an outsider. The advantage of that is we probably notice what others take for granted and see as commonplace. All the small things. I'm drawn to this place, this city. I could belong to it. There isn't, in any real sense, a comparison to be made with Perth. Indeed few people here know anything about our little town, and certainly don't know where it is. If they read it had fallen to some enemy it would not perturb them. But I was an outsider there, too, in a way. I never really belonged. My early upbringing, I suppose. A kind of schizophrenia. Come back here, and we will find somewhere and work here.

It is an odd chance I come to be here at all. We were all on our way to some destination unknown when I became ill and was offloaded here to hospital. I thought of Lieutenant Henry. For a time I seemed to worry them, a displaced cog in an invincible machine. I was placed temporarily as a clerk, and now in a guard pool, usually a prelude to further movement.

It's odd writing to someone who may never receive what you say. Perhaps it allows a kind of freedom, though this is not a personal letter. I am uncertain what hands it may go through. I probably shouldn't say I write it in a sparse kind of barracks. I stand in small sentry boxes. At gates. Outside cells. I've no idea what I'm keeping out. Did you find the fields of Arles?

It is not long before the women come. The voices go on, the talk, never silence here, as if that was somehow a disease in itself, but there are pauses, tension, at least on this day. The women's dresses

change everything, a colour, style, something
foreign to the uniforms of the week and the neutral
voices and the attitudes that hold in this place.
Different clothes that make clear the deadness, the
lack of real words, the dulling of memory that
grows all the week. The wife of the man next to
me, a big girl, plump, devouring, pulling a chair
against the bed and they are holding one another,
groping, the rest of the ward and our small world
well lost. The man spends his days here supposedly
with a nervous complaint. That, seeing him now,
is not surprising. One voice is unchanged, the
older man on the other side of the lovers. Perhaps
because of them, a little louder. His relatives, if in
fact he has any, are in another State. He never has
visitors. A voice that has offered us a life history no
one listens to any longer. Every day. It may even be
true. It is ordinary enough. If there is any excuse
for saying that. No one contradicts him. The
visitors carefully don't hear him. And the small
woman, very contained, has come and is sitting by
the bed near the end wall. Wife, sister, anything.
Nothing. She may be afraid. Each week he appears
to get a few hours leave, or takes it, homing in on
the brothels, tells us happily about it when he
comes back, falls into his bed, but after a time,
probably next morning, he is suddenly thrown on
the floor, thrashing, his body convulsed. In one
spasm he smashed his head through the asbestos
verandah, orderlies coming from everywhere.
Oddly, I have never found where they do come
from, we only see the nurses. They hold him. Yet
that seizure, that violence, is better somehow than
the stillness of the man whose bed is near the door,
passed by the nurses, the other patients, him seeing
none of them. Nor the quiet, well dressed woman

who on this day sits by him. There is a rumour
they will take him away for shock treatment. Or
perhaps they have already done. From that I doubt
anyone recovers. And I have to include myself
among this. A strange sweeping of casualties. Not
of this war. And not of anything this war will end.
I imagine you visiting me here. Now, seeing these
others. My bed very neat, undisturbed, a small
white bedspread precisely folded at the foot. But I
could not wish you in this place.

She heard him on the stairs, his quick run, he took them two at a time, light, easily. Across the narrow passage. She said: You're early.

Got to win sometimes.

I wouldn't be so sure.

I know, French. It's why I like you. No one easy sells you. We could go to Luna Park. I'll buy you an icecream.

More than one.

More than one.

Do you want to eat now?

Later. Let's get out of here.

She leaned towards the light by the mirror, making up her face carefully. Her shoulders and arms caught the light, were sharp, the angle of her shoulders, the hollow to her throat like shadow. He had not been sure she would take to the room. Alone a lot. Going down the road in the afternoon. Into town. She would not walk the city blocks, they go on for bloody ever, she said. Though she liked the shops. Would wander in them. She rode the trams. Going for a drink. Down the road Johnny at the Swan found her something to drink, even when it was short. The small room off the bar, dead and smoke filled and where he did not like going, could not breathe, she did not mind that. If that was her afternoon. She slept in the morning. It was what she was used to. If she brought men here in those afternoons there was no sign. And nobody would stop her if she wanted to. He touched the line of her shoulder blade.

You need food. Not icecream.

She put her hand over his. Icecream is food.

In the street there was no light. A man leaning on a half open gate spoke to them. She said: Nice night.

They walked quickly. He said: Why do you like them so much?

Like what?

Icecreams.

Them. You've got to like something.

He held her arm. I never thought of that.

In the warm night the stalls were crowded, they moved slowly, he won a doll throwing at the turning heads. You're good at that, she said. She had eaten the first icecream. He bought her another, and in one of the narrow walks two uniformed figures, girls hanging to them, bumped him, so that he went back against a railing. She stepped quickly, holding the icecream cone. Fast enough to avoid them. For a moment she saw his body tense. The sudden shaping as though it moved without his knowing. The figures moved on. He said: I could take those two.

She turned the cone gently. I thought you were going to.

I can't get into fights in this kind of place. The bloody police. MPs.

The high wheel turned above them. She licked the icecream carefully. They could pick you up for more than that, Harry.

Yes. But they won't.

No. They won't.

I get in strife down here I'm on my own. The police don't like getting involved all that much. But in this kind of brawl I'd be the one in the middle.

He stopped by a stall, put down his money, threw the balls hard, his body held. Nice going, the man said. Not another bloody doll, he said. I'll take the chocolates. If the box isn't empty. The man looking at him. French said: I'll take them. As they moved away he said: I'm not against the police. They do what they're told. They get their orders.

Are you going to fight over here?

I thought about it. At first. Three rounds. First on stuff. Any more than that and I'd be noticed. And I'd have to fight the way I'm told. No, I don't think they'd let me.

Just as well, she said.

I feel like it sometimes. Just get in there. Can't be worried. One more icecream and we'll see if we can find a place in this shit heap and feed you.

Thanks, she said. I can't wait.

The days of the guard pool are sometimes different, no more purpose than other days, but solitude. Hours off duty my own, and as long as I keep out of the way of officious lunatics I can be disregarded. So I can write to you, perhaps as some kind of attempt to find you. Odd fragments of this time stick in my mind, bits and pieces from the hours. Most is forgotten as if I had never done it. But some things. The boy who came up to a sentry box one afternoon, just on the edge of the city blocks. He had been selling papers and programmes. Covering a surprising distance through the streets. Wearing clothes cast off by some other child, too big for him, perhaps his brother's. He had had no lunch, there would not be anything at home, he would wait until tea time.

All matter of fact. It was raining slightly, a light drizzle with no wind to drive it, and the coke brazier was still alight. Some of the guards are fanatical in keeping it going, day or night, afraid of the cold. Or a point won against the accounting officers who work in here and expect it to be out in the daytime. Like an electric light they are paying for. The boy squatted down beside it, warming his hands. When next I looked he was asleep, huddled in the warmth. He woke suddenly and stood up and put his hand in his pocket as if I might have taken his money while he was asleep. Then he was gone. Somewhere down into those streets. The woman coming across the park at night. The place where I was stationed bordered on the edge of the park, it was late and the two figures were coming towards the pavement. There had been no one in there at night before. Not many gardens, trees that had lost their leaves. Then I could see the policeman, the woman dragging behind him, holding back, throwing herself away from him, but without any real effort and half running to keep up with him. As though it were a routine. It may have been. Already I can't be sure I saw that at all. It is the sound I remember, not arguing, not protesting, no words, hardly human, going on all the time with a sort of hopeless wailing. And yet it was not that. A keening. I can't describe it. The youth in the cells. Looking out the small square in the door at the light outside. Had never worked, existing somewhere down among the buildings of the edge of the city that you could see from one end of the corridor. Joining the services to avoid the police and going through and being caught and had got away. Now back in here, in these holding cells, for the official charade. And there has to be a guard on the cells. An unlikely guard, if he had broken away in the times he was moved outside I would have fallen over something. I don't know how far he would have gone. He kept asking the time. In those cells the walls alive with words.

 Women have children
 They have them with ease
 Trolls have bastards
 and call them MPs

 Singlet
 Shirt
 Sweater   Still bloody cold
 Overalls
 Sweater
 Overcoat
     Whoever thought of
      this guard business
     should be fucked with
     the end of a pineapple

 Remember Pearl Harbour
 Remember
 Cpl Smith
 F/O Jones   Always
 F/O West   Willing
 and many   After
 other bastards Sunset
 I will and God
 Help them later
 The war can't last for ever

      Wandering
      Around
      Australia
      After
      Fucks

The Prahan Madman
T.K.J.
27 Bendigo
27 Bendigo
27 Geelong
14 Geelong
14 Watsonia

    Oh Duty Officer do not weep
    the guard in here is not dead
    but only fast asleep

                     Tpr A.B.D.
                     45 Days AWL
                     6 months Pentridge

Pte K.E.R
Dubbo
Snatched From Freedoms Breast
alas Poor Me

               Some of these SPs would
               marry a prostitute and drag
               her down to his own level

    Young West
    alias
    Cpl E.B.   AAOC
      25 days Bendigo
    It's what you make it

Driver M.T.W
  9th Div Ammo Dump
  28 Days Bendigo
after having done 36 days Wayville
for AWL and Prison Break
      only 13 hours
        Bad Luck

Don't order any wood
I'm coming home with a load

   Driver A.Z
   Driver A.X
   1 Fraudelent Enlistment
   2 False statements
   3 AWL 17 months 27 days
    45 mins
    apprehended June at Wagga
   Sentence? 8 months July

Poor old reckless Andy
a bastard bold and bandy
They made him a guard
Just to get him randy.
Now with Ohms law
And Langes law and
even knock backs at the WAAF door
He's quite a dandy
Is poor old reckless Andy

  Pte XZ
  Donchester Showgrounds
   to
  Pucka
   to
  Palestine
   to
  Egypt
   to
  India
   to
  Ceylon
   to
  Singapore
   to

Fremantle
    to
Adelaide
    to
Here
    to
Richmond
    to
Royal Park
    to
Darly
    to
Richmond
    to
Royal Park
    to
Wangaratta
    to
Sydney
    to
Heidelberg
    to
Here
    to
Bendigo
  Back here
  Where next

Perhaps that one is not possible. But it should be. I may not be able to send you these. But I have to know what they are saying.

The light from the windows held the colour of the magazines, the low table. She said: It's a good place here, Jessica. You're lucky.

Yes. I suppose.

You know you are. There's just nowhere in Melbourne now.

As it happened my father knew someone.

Strange the people one's parents know.

Mine always seem to know people. Perhaps it was all those parties we used to have. Dinners. Weekends. But they are very good. I'd hardly afford this place myself, Joyce.

Their duty.

Even here, I don't know, I've never really got away from them, have I?

I don't see you have to get away from your parents.

You used to say I never would.

Perhaps I did. At school. But does it matter?

In early summer the creek dried to long pools. Some years seeming hardly to alter, until suddenly there was only the moist stained sand and the grey rocks. The water now deep. Joyce wading towards the bank, forcing the brown water ahead of her. You should come in, Jessie. It's not cold. Of course it's cold, she said. And someone might come. Joyce laughing, her hair sleek from the water. We should care. But she said: Someone would tell my parents. They can't do anything, Joyce said. Oh yes, they can disapprove. They're good at that. The girl standing firm, drawing the water up over her body, her strong shoulders, rubbing her hands up over her breasts, the thick nipples, blue veins clear under the skin. Don't Joyce, she said. You're a little prude, Jessie. What are you afraid of? Her hands held her breasts.

Charles is just like my parents, she said. He gets on so well with them. Particularly my father. Joyce, sometimes I think they both see me as a small girl.

Not very nice. I'm sure Charles isn't like that.

How would I know. But I'm glad you came. I miss seeing people I know.

You know a lot more people in Melbourne than I ever will. But I'm excited about this, Jessie.

Your horses. Very unpleasant deceitful things.

Trusting.

You were always sure about them, Jessica said. When we were at school. What you were going to do. Talking about them.

Yes. But then so were you. About clothes. But I wasn't sure you'd ever leave your house. Your beautiful house.

Two storeyed, stone, its wide front balcony where she liked to sit, but her mother said was too hot, too open to the sun and wind. The quiet rooms. Intimate, intimate in its silence, to sit in its rooms was to be aware of all sounds, of voices, movement. Lying over silence so that they were never forgotten. As a child listening, and wondering later they did not realise. Perhaps they did not care. Or a child could not matter. People coming to dine. The splendid dresses of the women. Parties on the lawn, by the heavy shrubs, the gardens. To stay overnight. Footsteps, heavy on the stairs. Laughter. Reminding her of the Boyd novels her parents liked to read, and which she did not care for, trying to read them because they wanted her to. But the house was more interesting.

It's what I miss, she said.

If John gets these horses he'll have a Clydesdale stud. To breed from. They're dying out, Jessie. Dead, just about.

And you're going off to Werribee to rescue them.

It's not a joke. He heard about this old man at Werribee was going to get rid of the horses he'd kept all through the last ten years. When everyone was getting rid of them. He's too old to look after them, and the bloody manpower people have taken his last man. Not producing food. So the man goes in the army and the Clydesdales go to the knackers. I'll drag the bloody manpower through all the horse shit I can find if they come near our place.

You could probably do it, Joyce.

Well, I've filled out, if that's what you mean. It's what my mother says. Bigger than ever. Who cares. No, I agree with John. It's mad to let them die out.

Are you going to marry John?

It's a Clydesdale stud, Jessie. We're not breeding people.

But would you?

I don't know. We help each other. I might marry him for the horses. Yes.

She stood by the window, looking at the narrow lane from the road, the high tree that shaded the side of the house and the pavement.

It's a lovely tree, Jessie. But you haven't looked at it, have you.

Of course. That's the side entrance. Lucky it's there. The old couple that own the house are deaf. They keep putting the chain on the front door. When I first came I was locked out for three hours. Now I have a key to the side door.

When you come in at night from dancing.

For when I come in.

It's strange you going to these servicemen's places, Jessie. I mean, I wouldn't have thought, oh, I don't know.

I like dancing. You know that. I've met some very good dancers. Some not. And people. Americans. Dutch. Negroes. New Zealanders.

Australians.

Australians.

They all want to come home with you. In the side door.

There is that. Not as much as you'd think. I mean, if you don't want to, it's okay.

And have you wanted to?

No.

But you have met someone.

In a way. But he's very strange. I don't know.
Really?
I think he could be in some kind of trouble. But it's not my business.
Which of all your nationalities does he fit?
Oh, he's an Australian.
Jessie if you go wandering about Melbourne in the blackout with very strange men you could end up a mess. You wouldn't be the first.
Not that way.
Strange any way would be enough.
Actually I feel very safe with him. And it's strange you go looking for Clydesdale horses with John in the middle of the war.
The magazines on the table, a page folded back at new designs, light from the window slanted across the sleek back of a model, the sharp colours of the covers. Clydesdales are important. They matter. Any time.
Do you think?
And anyhow, people are always going to want horses.
People are always going to want clothes.
People are. And you'll make more money, Jessie.

There were still empty tables. Men eating, a thin line at the cafeteria. Couples dancing. The band tired. Bored. Bored with the nights in here, this place that might have been a showroom, or below ground car park, the painted walls, the pillars. She was coming towards him, her plain white dress against the uniforms, her fair hair smooth, a neat blonde cap. Men looked at her, he watched them, she did not notice. Or care. She had never seemed to pose. Pretend. Drifted away somehow, and that was not a pose. As if she was unaware. Not hearing. As she could be unaware of this place, of noise, the men and women.
You look very serious, she said.
Jessica, he said. I was thinking about you.

I'm sorry if it makes you serious.
Not particularly serious.
And I'm late.
I thought you might not be here tonight.
I'm usually earlier. My girl friend has come down from the country. We're neighbours, actually. Grew up together. Went to boarding school. All that. She's staying with me. Would you like to meet her?
Should I?
Why not?
There are probably reasons. I don't know.
She'd like to meet you. She's with a friend who wants to buy some Clydesdale horses.
Is he staying?
Of course not. They're going to see this old man at Werribee. He's worse about horses than she is.
The old man?
Her friend. You don't have to confuse me.
I'm not.
He has a property out past hers. I think Joyce is more interested in the Clydesdales than in him. He's a stubborn sort of person. I never did get on with his family much.
Out where your property is. Your house.
How did you know about that?
You told me.
I don't remember.
I don't think you do. Probably. But you've mentioned it quite often.
Perhaps I did. I like the house very much.
We had a team of Clydesdales, he said. A few were a bit suspect, but they had the blood. My father wouldn't sell them for slaughter. He turned them out. They broke a few fences. And they ate a lot of feed. There were three left last time I was there.
I'm glad, she said. Glad of that. Was it very long since you were there?

A few lifetimes. One at least.
You don't say anything about those sort of things.
No.
Will you go back there after the war?
No, he said. Do you want to dance?
Yes. Please. She went ahead of him, onto the space divided from the tables, the line of the cafeteria, along one side the stage for the band. She said: Is that why you come here?

I come here because there is a very reasonable cafeteria and a decent place to eat.

Oh. I see.

I knew a girl wanted to be a dancer. Once.

Really? And did she?

I doubt it.

There's a better dance place we could go to on a Saturday, she said. If you like.

You're the dancer. Obviously very good. You're so light. I don't know you're there.

I know.

What does that mean?

Nothing. Would you like to?

We could try. Is this before or after I meet your friend?

I'd forgotten. Come to dinner tomorrow night. Can you do that?

I don't know, he said. About either. I can't be sure.

I understand.

No. Things are changing for me.

You won't be coming here.

I might not.

Will you be going away?

I don't know.

We're not supposed to ask questions. I shouldn't have asked that.

In fact I don't know.

You could always ring me. We could go to a film.

That might be better.
And if you want to come tomorrow night. It's not hard to find. Do you know South Yarra?
Hardly. I'm a stranger in these parts.
I'll draw a plan on this envelope. Do you have a pencil?
I'm sorry.
Then you'll just have to remember.

There was no one behind the small counter. A cubicle just inside the door. An entrance hall, or passage. To the left swing doors, half glass, opaque, sweeping curves and arabesques, some minor screen for the bar. A man came from the passage, he did not at first see him, short, heavy, a thin cardigan over a white shirt, grey trousers.
Yes?
He was not sure the man had spoken. I was looking for a room.
A room.
Yes.
For long?
I'm not sure.
Not sure.
I'm going to work not far from here. I'm trying to find somewhere to live.
You thought here.
It was near the tram junction. I saw the place while I was waiting.
We don't do board. Only breakfast. It's the staff. You can't get anyone.
That wouldn't matter.
From behind the counter the man took down a key. He opened a register.
You can sign that. But it's in advance.
The room opened off the end of the long upstairs passage. At the top of the stairs there was the short angle of another passage. The room not much wider than the

passageways, a single window, a lane below and a brick wall, blackened, dirt or old paint. The narrow bed, a washstand, high narrow wardrobe.

You will want breakfast?

Yes, he said.

In the narrow room at night a silence. The occasional voices below, where the bar was. Closed. Footsteps on the stairs and along the short angle of passageway. Going down the stairs in the evening he had seen one of the women, thin, short dark hair, black dress. Night. On the stairs. In whatever rooms those were. In the first few nights he slept heavily, if the sounds woke him, it was not unpleasant. Almost welcome. To go back to sleep. Though the mornings were different.

The street was deserted. Already shadowed. The phone box, a heavy stench, smoke, a kind of ammonia, urinal. In that street there may have been no other. He traced his finger over the glass. Not knowing if it would be her voice. You won't remember me. She said: Why yes. Of course I do. She said yes we could go to a film. You can choose, he said. At the Town Hall then. Looking at his clothes, quickly, making no comment. Things have changed, he said. Is that better? I don't know, he said. I don't think so. Afterwards, in the coffee shop she took him to, he said: Do you still go dancing?

I haven't been. You?

No.

Have you been away?

Another country. I've been ill again. A kind of physical absurdity. I don't know why.

Do we know why we are ill?

I suspect so.

And now it is different.

It is like changing cells, he said. I don't think this one is any better. It may be less honourable. Though I don't

know that's a word I like using.
   Can I ask what it is you do?
   I work in a small and rather dirty office. A kind of design and calculator place. Mathematical checking. Working out. All approved by the holy powers.
   And you don't like it. Obviously.
   It is obvious.
   I'm sorry.
   The problem is not so much my not liking it. It's that I don't think I should have accepted it. A wrong choice.
   But you would not have had any choice?
   I did have.
   I don't understand.
   I'm sorry. I didn't mean to go into all this.
   Well I'm glad you have come back from your other country. Wherever it was.

He woke slowly, and he heard the woman laugh, the heavy steps on the narrow stairs. Where if he passed either of the women he had to stand back against the wall. Their heavy scent. The room. I can't write there, he said. I don't know why. Nothing. It's like a kind of insulation. She said: It seems a very odd place. Not really. I didn't think I'd still be there. I can't afford it. But the two women use rooms there. And that can't be much of a secret. They'd be paying someone up the ladder. Though it's a curiously deserted part, not much traffic. Not a lot of people. And there'd have to be people in the bar some nights. I don't know what that's about. I don't go near. She said: Do people stay there? A few, he said. They show up in the morning for breakfast. Then they're usually gone. She said: It sounds like a kind of underworld place. It is an underworld, he said. And I can't write about it. I don't know why. It's all around me. It may be your work. It may be. That you hate so much. And I'm sorry we had to see such a bad film. Neither are your fault, he said. So don't be sorry. It will work out. She touched the coffee cup, not lifting it, her fingers tracing the thick curve. Do you go with the women? Do I go with them? No I don't. Maybe that's why you can't write about the place. If it is, he said, there are things I don't have to do for art. She lifted the cup. It's good coffee. For a change. I'm glad of that. Glad of the good coffee? Glad about your art. Though I've nothing against the women, he said. I rather like them. I don't know any people like that, she said.

The building was old. It was hard to talk to the man. Held briefly in the small entrance cubicle. Yes. Old, the man said. She's been here a long time. There were few words. Anything he said taken down and used in evidence. As perhaps it had. The dark stone and brick, at one end fretted, a side wall rendered, some long dead words faded, without context.

   ALES AND STOUTS

      PLAYERS PLEAS

    GOLDEN FLAKE

   DE WITTS KIDNEY & BLADDER

  INDIAN ROOT PILLS

     HIS MASTER'S VOICE

Not old enough, however thinned, for those days when there had been places like this, the streets filled, horses, waggons, the sulkies and traps, men carrying their possessions through the mud, stepping around the potholes. The rooms filled, beds on the floors, the tables. Noise. Or was it old enough. Its passage floors were worn, the wooden doors, the panellings had known enough hands. Wood smoothed and with a kind of ingrained dirt so that it was natural. In places painted. I can't afford the place, he said. Though it's cheap enough. I should be trying to save. She said: Why do you want to save? I can never get used to your questions, he said. They are very odd. In the office with its partitioned spaces, the desks, cabinets, and shelves, a disorder, deliberate, controlled. Difficult to penetrate. Long tables with drawing instruments. Lights. Though in the rest of the space that might once have been a display floor, lighting sparse enough. You don't want to see too much, one of the men said.

Heavy clouds dulled the water, the ponds, small lakes. The grass deep in colour and the massed beds of flowers, the thick shrubberies, high clumps of trees he did not recognise, had never seen. Its own jungle. Von Mueller walking here, planning. Collecting, in places where few enough men had ever been. No bad memorial, here, this, to a life's interest, an enthusiasm. Dulled, it was said, at the end, and the gardens given to the care of others. Still no matter. They had more chance, those people who were here early. She was coming from the entrance, walking quickly, a light brown coat, no hat. She said: It is cold.
   Cold. I've been guarding this bench.
   She sat beside him. Her pale skin had a colour from the cold. She said: It's strange being here. You are not at work.
   No.
   I'm sorry. That was a stupid question.
   Was it a question?

In a way.
No, he said. I am not at work.
Have you had lunch?
I hadn't thought about it.
I have something. Fruit. An apple, this pear. It's very messy. Which do you want?
It's like offering food to the animals at the zoo.
Is it?
The pear. I wouldn't like you to spoil your coat.
Do you like it?
It's very handsome.
You have left that place. I knew you would.
I can't stay there, he said. There's a kind of obscenity about it. I've been trying to make a decision. It will be the wrong decision.
Can I ask why?
It's made too late. It's probably a vicarious decision. If you can have one of them.
I've hardly ever been here, she said. It's beautiful.
I'm not sure how I got here. I was just walking. I should have gone to a bar for the day.
Would you have phoned me if you had?
Probably not.
Then it's just as well. Does this mean you will be leaving your old hotel?
It will mean that.
You like that place.
Not like. But something. It has some kind of hold. I think about it a great deal. And I can't use it.
Are your women still there?
Hardly mine. Yes. They'll always be there. Unless there's a change of control somewhere. In whatever hierarchy.
That's sad.
It's not sad. It's survival.
I don't understand you when you're like this.

Jessica, he said. It's not a good day. And it's cold. I shouldn't keep you here.

Will I see you again?

It's not like that.

You can always call me.

In your shop. Is it warm there?

She looked at the dark water. She placed the apple core carefully in the paper bag.

Most of the time.

This letter can be added to those I may not send you. Though I seem to have sent most. I have to have someone to talk to. It's the old cliche. I have never seen so many people as live in this city, yet I can't talk to anyone. I have managed to get to art exhibitions, as I told you, met some painters, a few people who write. All this at present a kind of casual acquaintance, though I like some of the painters. But I suppose you were the only person I did talk to in any real sense, and then it was less a matter of saying a great deal than of understanding one another. However, events have taken an odd turn. Near what might have been the end of my stint as a guard of the establishment I became ill again. This time involved endless tests and they didn't seem to know what to do with me. I had none of the proper mutilations of war. In the end I was released to a manpowered job to work for someone who had the right contacts. And of course defence contracts. Always defence. My early work with figures, such as banking, no doubt, and being able to manipulate formulae and other processes I have no interest in must have decided them. The work had a monumental dullness, indeed it made banking exhilarating, but the attitude in the place defeated me. I don't often dislike people more or less at once. Or I didn't think I did. My employer and I achieved that. I think he was happy about that, because he had power over me and I suppose the others in his establishment. I've always tried to avoid people I don't like. Not combat them. I could not avoid them in this place. A little hierarchy of people having to hold jobs that kept them safe and well. I'm the last to blame them for that. But resentful of any newcomers. In fact afraid of them. I could do little right for the chief-owner-manager everything and anything he may be. I told him I had better go. He said he could see I did not do that. He likes his show of power. I don't know if he could have. Or if I would have been found some other profiteering establishment. Ironically my only skills seem to lie that way. It seemed to me that a little work on the books, a quick audit of certain aspects, might have been embarrassing for him. But then, probably not, since no doubt money found its way upwards and he was well protected. I got in the tram as usual to go to work in the morning, an all very commonplace day, and found myself walking about in the streets of the city. I went and sat in the Gardens for a time. Very much as we used to. Once. I had an idea I might talk it into some kind of reason with a friend, but that didn't happen. It was cold and going to rain. I went up to the Public Library and I stayed there and the day passed. I went to see Harry. I do not now exist. But I am not alone in that.

Those bastards, Harry said. You're well out of that. Sleep here. Till things settle down. You can use the couch.

Couch, French said. Is that what it is.

The girl sitting at one end of the couch touched the faded floral cover. It would be better than what's at my place.

Leslie doesn't need a couch, Harry said. She has a bed. I have to go out. Only about an hour. Bring your things over here.

In the street he walked with the girl in the darkness. At the corner she said: I catch the tram here. Will you work for him?

No, he said. Unless it works out that way. Do you?

Me? I go there sometimes to see French. No. I work on my feet. Saves my back. Come in the cafe sometime for a meal.

He had been uncertain. But a place to eat. In the early evening the cafe crowded, shift workers, a few casuals, men who talked among themselves, noticed strangers. As they had observed him. Seldom women. Reasonably clean, the food little varied, but always enough. At first commonplace, but almost sinister. As if the commonplace, the ordinariness, was a set deliberately contrived. A piece of social realist theatre. Someone to come in off the street. The tables hushed. A place guarded by those who used it. They're all right, Leslie said. They don't say much. Like you, he said. She laughed. Nothing to say around here.

Standing by the table, the cafe quiet, the tables cleared, he was late and thought she might have gone. She said: You're not still at Harry's. They moved.

No, he said. I helped them. Not that there was that much to shift. No. I'm in a place down the road. Temporary.

French has wanted a bigger place. Somewhere they can cook, get meals.

Sometimes I don't think she cares.

Who does. She has problems. I like French.

Yes, he said. So do I. Though I'm not sure she's ever seen me.

The girl laughed. I know what you mean. Harry can handle her. She drew her fingers along the table, a long arc. We could have a drink. I'm going now.

They walked the few blocks. It's not far, she said. She opened the wooden gate, lifting, the panels uneven. Don't push it, she said. The bloody thing might fall down. And it makes a noise. There were heavy shrubs about the path. She walked quickly in the darkness, along the side of the house, he thought she had gone inside but she said: Down here. Not the house.

He bumped against her and she took a key from her handbag. In the room she closed the door, turned on the light. He calls it a room, she said.

He?

The old bastard. In the house. Are you okay?

A few problems at the moment. Tired mainly.

She watched him hold the glass she had found from the littered table. You don't have to drink it. You don't look all that good. Maybe a cup of tea would be better.

No, he said. I'm sorry.

She drank quickly. It's all there is.

Harry?

No. Finish it. There could be more where that came from.

She stood up slowly, slipping the dress from her shoulders. She fumbled in the small wardrobe, her arms white in the thin light from the globe.

You don't like it, she said. Maybe it's the water makes it like that. Forget the drink idea.

On the bed she said: I'm clean, lover. I'm all right.

I must be tired.

In the morning she said: The customers don't usually complain.

Did I complain?

Maybe I should.

I'll get you a cup of tea. That we didn't have last night. While you think about it.

She lay, her knees drawn up, hunched, watching him look for things on the crowded shelf and table against the wall. When he brought the cup she said: You have uses. Do you have somewhere to go? Work?

Not now. No.

Stay here. Sleep. You look like you could do with it. I'm off this afternoon. See you then.

When he woke she was standing just inside the narrow doorway. The curtains drawn. The room dark. I was right, she said. I brought us something to eat.

In the mornings the small room was shadowed, dark. Don't use the light, Leslie said. He'll see it. Okay if I'm here. The garage at the end of the narrow path obscured by garden shrubs, rich leafed, red, yellow veined, fleshy. At times in the early morning, the curtains drawn to a slit, the heavy leaves softening the light, he looked into what had been a garden. Don't let the bloody light in, she said. It's too early. A door gave onto the lane, set in a larger door, long boarded up, the garage once opening to the laneway, its walls daubed with paint, fused words.

PIGIRON

                  FIGHT THE BILL

KILL

                  BULLDOGS

     No Conscription

                            ROSE FUKS

Broken fences leaned into the narrow space, boards torn off and thrown down. Gathered for firewood. At night voices, a child crying, someone running. The door was stripped of paint, the wood splintered, the softwood whorled and knotted. It's the best way, she said. But be careful. The old bastard has the house knows he can't let this. It's got fuck all. The council would have him. So he doesn't ask questions as long as there's no trouble. He must know I'm here, he said. He might not. He doesn't come out the back much. He doesn't want to know.

At times, at night, at first, she brought someone back to the room. She gave him time, speaking before she opened the door from the path at the back of the house. While he went without sound into the lane. Like some cinema comedy. The doors opening. Closing. To walk the streets that were oddly deserted. Without light. Without traffic. The broken lines of buildings, as if abandoned, decaying. Rarely, a door opening abruptly onto light, so that he held back, to the shadows. Once, early, a heavy fog, and he lost his way, went back, found the corner.

You're a funny bastard, she said. Lying on the bed, the thin covers pushed back. She seemed thin, in her clothes, the rather ordinary dresses of her day time or her work, but naked with a symmetry of body he found hard to describe. Why do you look at me like that?

I was trying to put you in words. You have a very fine body.

She drew the covers up about her shoulders. It's sure not for this I keep you here.

You don't need me for this. You're not short, are you?

No. But it is a bit funny. I've never had anyone stay here before.

I haven't had to go on my night walks lately.

No. That was money.

I don't have money.

We have enough between us to eat. But I don't know

how it happened.

I get your breakfast.

In the mornings she wanted to sleep. Whatever the night had held. He made tea, she would not drink coffee, hated the ersatz he could get from Harry, a piece of toast, they seldom had butter. At times she brought some from the cafe. He waited until she woke, to eat with her. He kept the small sink space, the few shelves, the table, tidy, making a parcel of empty jars and cartons that she said could not have come from the room and was unwilling to put in the bin at the side of the house. Drop it down the end of the lane in the dark, she said.

There'll be a bin along one of the streets. There'd have to be.

I wouldn't bet on that. Not round here. She rolled over on the bed, stretching, her body lifting in an arc, flopping back. You'll go when you're ready, she said.

Or when you are.

Another brick path from the house curved past the shrubs to a lavatory, close to the garage, the bricks broken, the gaps covered in a soft green moss. As if no one walked the path. Yet he was uneasy, to be caught in the small cold lavatory. Shaded by the heavy shrubs that seemed forgotten. Like the spreading bamboos and the lillies at the back of his aunt's house, with its own small, similar cell. His aunt standing in the passage before the curtain. I am sorry you are going. I do not believe in these wars. I will not interfere with your room. If you wish to come back. Leslie said: Don't worry. I do, he said. He's going to find me there sometime. Trapped. She laughed. He won't see you, she said. He doesn't shit. At night, before he went to bed, the lane at the back.

When he could no longer work, in the late afternoons, he went in to the city, at times ringing Jessica, at the number she had given him, the shop he had never seen, that he pieced together from the images of places glimpsed about the city streets. She enjoyed films, was interested in the clothes, the costumes of lavish dance sets. Ideas, she said. Design. But they're all the same, he said. She laughed. You wouldn't know. They had coffee in a shop in Elizabeth Street, near the station. The night streets half lit, crowded. The streets are best in the early morning, he said. A beautiful city. A kind of mist. Fog sometimes. You're being sarcastic, she said. That's not kind. No, he said. It has great beauty. She caught the tram and he went back through the city. Along the lane to the back door. It's not the back, Leslie said. It's the front door to this place.

In the mornings she washed from a basin, gasping at the cold, standing naked on the thin mat over the cement floor. Sponging under her arms, between her legs. God I stink. Give me the bloody powder. He forced the thin towel over her, reddening her clear skin, at times she said: No I won't, and jumped back into bed. When she was warm she tried to dress sitting up in the bed. It's not bloody fair. I feel the cold. She went, as he did, not often, down to the public baths. It's too far, she said. And who cares.

His books made a small row along the window sill. If I open the window they'll all go, she said. He looked at the thin line. But you won't open the window. She picked up a book from the table. *Housing The Australian Nation*, she said. It's not real. You don't read this crap. Her way of reading the titles to him, clumsily, made a satirical comment he enjoyed, but he said: Well look inside the thing, and she put the book down. I don't read. Can't he said. She ran her finger along the back. Don't.

A lot of these things are communist stuff. She looked at the book backs in the light from the window, curtained, a Sunday. She slept all Sunday morning, a ritual he never disturbed, making tea for them both when she pushed herself from the still neat bedclothes.

Published by left groups, he said. Are you going to

drink this in bed?

Yes. Why left groups?

Who else cares.

You should be careful.

He opened a packet of sweet biscuits and she said: When did you get those?

Harry. With his regards. When I saw him yesterday. You'd have eaten them if I'd told you.

I did eat a packet once. Of those.

I don't believe that.

It's only sweet things. I don't care about food.

No, he said. I'm not a communist. I'm no sort of ist. Life would be easier if I was. But I agree with some of what they stand for.

If you were ever in strife, they could be bad for you. This sort of thing.

Are you talking about the books?

Yes. And Harry's mob wouldn't like them that much.

They're not in a language Harry's mob read. Or speak that much, some of them.

She held out the empty cup to him. There's some bad buggers among them. Why do you work for him?

Some highly respected men, you mean. I don't work for him. He got me a job answering phones on Saturdays. I run a few messages. I have to have money. A message boy.

It's the boys get hurt, she said. You should be careful.

He opened the lane door so that a narrow line of light angled across the grey floor, the edge of the mat.

I am. Why don't we go for a walk in the Gardens?

If we can catch a tram, she said. And you massage my shoulders. To get me started. I'm tired.

The things that get you started.

You're good at this, she said. His fingers spreading the flesh across her shoulders, the base of her neck. Along the curve of her back. Maybe I'll just stay here.

The building had been a warehouse, standing clear of its neighbours on three sides, some land around it vacant, weed covered. At one end close to the houses that stretched away in a pattern he had not tried to resolve. Old furniture, crates, bundles of covered parcels that were never moved filled the lower part of the building, a pathway along the wall at the end to stairs up to the loft. Small windows made the upper space light, a door that opened to the yard below bolted across. A good exit gone, Jackson said. A pot belly stove in the centre of the floor. The walls layered with sheets of hardboard, cardboard, smoothed wood. He could walk along the walls, moving the finished or abandoned paintings, like looking through books on a stall, he said. I paint them over, Jackson said. No one wants them. Dark, shuttered paintings, figures in broken streets and buildings, held outside the houses he passed on his way to the studio, figures of half seen streets. There was little light, the colours sombre, browns, blacks, unexpected richness in the shadows. In the faces, half seen, carved like the houses and streets. The secret of these faces stone. Yes, Jackson said. But there's a fair amount of old wood and galvanised iron around. You shouldn't paint them over, he said. Jackson seemed not to hear. Then he said: A few survive. Enough to show when there's somewhere to show them. Take one. I can't do that, he said. I insist, Jackson said. You have some feeling for what I'm doing. Anything except that big one. That has to go to George Edmonds.

Leslie said: God.

You don't like it.

I work among that mob. I don't want them back here. My private life. Please.

Jackson might see that as a compliment.

Just so I don't have to look at it. Turn it round.

When she had gone to work he faced the painting out to the small room, the crowded dark figures, the taut faces taking what light the room held, drawing it to them. Strong. Hard. Before she came back he turned it to the wall. I haven't had one revolve before, Jackson said. I should meet the girl.

In the half light of the cinema the shadows were clear and shifted plainly, with accuracy, definition, before them. I've come by a painting, he said. I'd like you to see it. But she did not hear, absorbed. Still. Beside him. As they went out she said: Did you like it?

Not much. Very heroic. People seemed to approve.

I thought it was brave. In a way. Sad.

All those men splashing about in a tub of water somewhere. Sound effects. Battleships everywhere. Yes. I suppose it was.

What did you say about a painting? Did you mean the film?

No.

What then?

I've come by a painting. It doesn't matter.

It does, doesn't it. Could I see it?

Sometime, he said. It might be awkward just now.

Is it where you live?

Yes.

And I can't see it there.

Jessica I can't take people there. I could show you other paintings like the one I have. One afternoon. Can you walk out on the job?

Probably.

She was standing just inside the doorway. As if suddenly she was afraid. Her hands clasped about the white handbag. People moved about the room, some talking at one of the tables, voices quickly raised. He thought she did

not see him. He said: Jessica.
　She said: I couldn't come earlier.
　Are you all right?
　Of course.
　I thought you looked tired.
　No. I haven't been here before.
　It's not as bad as all that. He touched her arm, moving her forward, her arm for a moment stiff, her body held against him. Against movement. She said: It is very crowded.
　There's not so many here now.
　I mean, all the paintings. I don't think I expected so many.
　It's a kind of shock. Not your conventional gallery thin line. You come in here and it's just something you don't expect. Or I didn't. The first exhibition I saw here, I simply wasn't prepared for it. A vitality. A kind of mad vitality. But purpose. Relevance. Whatever you like. It's not something that lived in my part of the world.
　I didn't know it lived here.
　The walls alive. Dark streets, people huddled, the faces, hard, deprived, light suddenly along a broken wall, and the darkness of blacked out streets, the moving forms of shadows, sharp light against blackness, life and darkness. Swirling tortured landscapes and figures he did not understand. Massed abstraction. Paintings with nothing in common. Yet everything. Painters whose names he had never known. Barbara you were wrong. It is here. You should be here. If anything is to come it will come from here.
　It's another world, he said. Something you suddenly find.
　I don't know that I like them very much.
　Liking is not really relevant.
　It would be for me. If I was to buy something like this. A painting.

I doubt if many of these people paint that way. I mean, to sell their work.
 Is that irrelevant too?
 In one sense. Yes.
 I still don't think it is for me.
 If someone does buy, good.
 They are rather uncomfortable things. Some of them frighten me. Those war figures. The destruction. Dark. Greenish. I mean, everything has gone. It does frighten me.
 Despair. And mockery. Irony. That is more frightening.
 Yes.
 A gum tree is better.
 Oh yes. If you are going to have to live with it. Is the painting you told me you had like these?
 Along here. Jackson. He's got three paintings here.
 Oh.
 Yes.
 I don't know. I don't think I'd want to design dresses, have them all made up, if I didn't think anyone would want them.
 You'd have some so-called critics on your side in not liking these. This exhibition has been reviewed as an unpleasant jolt. The critic's words. Exceedingly unwholesome, one reviewer called it. He said these paintings reflected a morbid viewpoint that filled him with despair. And disgust. It was a chamber of horrors. Oddly, he didn't say what the world outside was like.
 You know I don't think that.
 We should all be out in Collins Street singing Rule Britannia.
 I'm sorry I don't like this. For your sake.
 What does that have to do with it?
 Because you like them. Because they mean a lot to you.
 You're extraordinary, he said.
 In her white sleeveless dress, her arms white, slender,

her hands held about the plain white handbag, her hair smooth. Held back from her face, elegant, and he was surprised at the word.

And you're beautiful. People look at you.

She stared at the dark night street, the harsh pool of light, the heavy figures at its edge. Their shoes are in the light, she said.

The painting stood against the wall, half held in light from the high window. David William said: You're a realist, Jackson. Social realist. You always will be. The worm is in you.

I don't know, Jackson said.

If you go anywhere it'll be into expressionism. And we know what happens to them.

Possibly. I'm some way there anyhow.

The painting may have worked less well than he expected. There might have been some stylizing in the streets and buildings and people, perhaps the faces drew the painter back. And William's influence might have been responsible. In part. If Jackson listened to him. To anyone. This painting like a story forced to a wrong conclusion. William's own painting overflowed the crowded back verandah and part of a shed at the back of his family's home further away in Carlton. A house secluded, shielded by larger buildings on either side, turned in from the street, crowded by a family that showed no sign of leaving its shelter for an outside world. A somehow savage group. Not noisy, determined in their privacy and whatever kind of relationships were fought out in the few rooms. The younger brothers, the sisters, two of them older, the silent parents. When he went there with Jackson they looked at him, and did not offer or decline any welcome. That mob, Jackson said. I don't go there too often. David's never been involved outside. The bloody war. I don't think he went to school. He doesn't exist. Anyone goes in there and there are that many bodies all directions it never makes sense. Enough of them are official. Must be. They've got coupons. Work when they want it. Like one of David's paintings. All bloody upside down.

Figures hung upside down in odd landscapes that held crowds in streets and always a few solitary figures walking away to some place that lay beyond those houses and those streets. Some of the tidily stacked boards were tranquil suburban landscapes, empty, the figures gone, the buildings in folds of rich colour. The Boyds get through to him at times, Jackson said. I think he had a Boyd period. But he could only feel a conviction in the images that denied influence.

We'll go out to George Edmonds' one Sunday, Jackson said. He's a collector. You should meet him. A shrewd bastard, but he's helped a few of us.

He's a speculator, William said. He's not helping us. He's an accountant.

He'll have a long wait on yours, Jackson said. He's helped me stay in this place.

They'll pull it down after the war. He'd buy it if he thought he could get a good offer later.

I'd buy it. I don't want it wrecked. I like the place.

Of course it could fall down, William said. Save a lot of trouble.

The house was large, more recent than he had expected, wide glass windows at the front. So he can see the garden, William said. He's more interested in that than painting. A formal garden, in streets of formal gardens, the care, he thought, of paid gardeners rather than individuals. Safe. Predictable. The rooms bare, functional in furnishing that surprised him and he had seen only in illustrations, wall space for paintings, one long room given over to a gallery. He may be pissed, William said. He has a few bad weekends. Depends on his wife. But he thought Edmonds seemed quiet, almost nervous, yet in looking at the paintings, talking of them, had an authority, a certainty.

Edmonds foraged in the kitchen for a late meal, talking about writing and painting, offering to introduce him to a publisher and some of those interested in new writing. Edmonds had a certain detachment, as if in all that he talked of he was knowing, aware, yet uninvolved. Without, it seemed, passion. What's funny? Jackson said. An echo, he said. Later in the evening Edmond's wife came in, with a painter she had been helping arrange an exhibition. You must see it, she said. Quite splendid. He could not find the tension William seemed convinced existed between her and Edmonds. She talked a good deal, rapidly, with fire at times, she and Edmonds were relaxed, easy with one another. She was a big woman, taller than Edmonds, expensively dressed, some of her husband's businesses found a purpose in things other than art. David William curiously uneasy with her. Edmonds drove them to the station. The painter with the exhibition did not come with them. Piss artists, William said. All of them.

The road held a few trees along its edges, beyond the roadside cleared paddocks, broken clumps of trees. Lousy country, Jackson said.

Roberts and Streeton country, William said. Give in a few miles.

Jackson said: I'm not sure about this house. You should see it. There's quite a bit of talk about it. He's built it into the landscape.

Not your kind of landscape, William said.

Not my kind of house. But interesting.

He's used natural materials, the natural landscape. Effective. It may be a bit forced. But strong. I tried to paint it.

That's the one came out as a cow paddock, Jackson said.

There's a movement towards this kind of thing, Edmonds said. I don't think I share the conception.

The early start, in Edmonds car, William's idea. He's got petrol, William said. That's one car won't be on blocks. You can't go anywhere this early, Leslie said. Stay here. I'd rather, he said. But they expect me. He did not know why William had made the suggestion, forcing Edmonds, who showed no enthusiasm his visit, journey, business trip, whatever it might have been, should be shared. There was an antagonism between the two men he did not understand. If Edmonds would go so far as antagonism. These bare paddocks. The few houses. Edmonds' careful garden.

Beyond a turn in the road he saw the house. Soil gouged from the side of a rise, the house set close to the walls of the cavity, like a cave, its own walls stone and mud brick. Along the bare rise deep runnels cut the soil. The trees near the house cut for timber. A few stumps along the crest of the rise.

Inside, the stone surfaces made the room dark. Mud brick walls splashed a deep yellow. Spaces of rough stone. There were few paintings, those he saw seemed confused and uncertain. Edmonds and the painter, Kurt, it seemed, no one called him anything else, walked outside for a time. Other people came, there were two flagons of wine, little to eat. The voices filled the long front room that was the studio. He looked out the windows fitted carelessly to a rock sill and there was the bare ground and the stumps along the slope, a thin dry grass.

Leslie said: I thought you were lost. Did you enjoy it?

Not really, he said. We stayed longer than I thought.

I've been asleep all day, she said. Great.

Jackson walked with a limp that was curiously irregular. When I think of it, he said. The man who shot himself in the foot. Actually some fucker in an army lorry ran over it.

The leg. Broke it about. Their doctors didn't help that much. But it got me out. The whole thing worried me and I had a few turns. Bit unreal looking back on it. I got into the psycho ward. I thought I was going out the hard way then. The bastards were using shock treatment. I saw poor sods as good as killed by that. If they thought you weren't genuine they'd keep you at it till you broke. I think they were using the whole thing as an experiment. They didn't put me through that. They reckoned I was useless and scrapped me. For a while I couldn't sleep thinking about that place. I couldn't get enough grog so I used to work. One day I might do a series on it. Not now. I don't want to remind them I'm still around.

He was never sure Jackson would be at the studio. Jackson worked for a small printer, in broken periods, at times day and night, at others a few hours. I can get you a few jobs collecting stuff, Jackson said. Slave rates. But no questions. Yes, he said. If you can. The key of the studio was in a cleft of the heavy door frame. Turning the paintings at one end of the room, where they were obscured by shadow, he found one at first unfamiliar, only a faint suggestion of the streets and buildings of Jackson's work, streets here distant and fading, unclear, lost in shadow, dominated by the heavy foreground, a room, cell, three white figures, their faces turned away, anonymous, the bars of a window heavy, black, a figure on the plank bed, lost in other shadows of the standing shapes. Black smears of graffiti on the walls. He was looking at it when Jackson came in. Private, Jackson said. He turned it away into the shadow.

It is mainly city painting, if I can call it that.
People. Everywhere. The city in decay. It's not just

war. Some of this painting goes back all through the last ten years, though you and I didn't see it. And I certainly never realised it was happening. I don't understand it all. Some I doubt there is anything to understand. I don't like all of it. But I am growing to it. There's an extraordinary activity now. You should be here. Would it be possible to find a way back here now? Does anyone get through the lunacy? It is said numbers of quite harmless and decent internees are being brought here. So perhaps. I like this city very much now. Still, and perhaps for ever, an outsider, but I feel it about me. A city self contained. Which it isn't. The red dust blows down from the mallee. All a kind of inner landscape, nothing outside. Two painters whose work seems to me very striking indeed, took me to see an odd sort of house gouged out of the earth by a European exile, I suppose he was. One of the sensitive people who are to educate us raw colonials in the finer matters of taste. My painter friends thought it demonstrated some unity of building and Australian landscape. Our farm house that you painted has more unity with its landscape than this had. Sometimes I think there is not even much real awareness of history, though there is a richness of it here. For instance, thinking of landscape, there is more affinity with landscape in John Batman's two huts so finely drawn in Bonwick's *Port Phillip Settlement* than these late concoctions. I've been reading the book in the Library. The sketches in it, and the drawings like those in Sherer's *Gold Finder*, I wish I could talk about with you. Odd, that in my so called education, while I remember some vaunted European battles, and a few English kings, no one mentioned Bonwick or John Batman. But then I don't remember anyone mentioning Stirling either. Barbara, you have been trapped by this mad emphasis on what is in fact a foreign country. You should be here. There is a lot of painting that somehow you must see. It's tremendously rich. Makes a mockery of the kind of contemporary painting we used to see. Painters we didn't know. Or I didn't. Tucker, Boyd, Counihan, Nolan, Perceval, Bergner. Some women painters, Jacqueline Hick, a few things I've seen of Joy Hester. Why haven't we ever seen their work? But you would find yourself here. I suppose I can say that. It's probably true you always had found yourself. Let it go. I've met a number of painters here, more than I have or seem likely to of writers. The painting impresses me more, it's so far ahead of writing. It doesn't matter if you don't answer these letters. Perhaps this is a kind of diary. You would have to send anything to the name and address I've given. No other. I'll explain one day.

It's your day off, he said. We should go somewhere.
I don't have days off.
You do. Even if you don't get them.
It's too early.
Why don't we go to the zoo?
The zoo? I work in a bloody zoo.
Have you ever been?
No. I'm happy about that.
I'll go out and get something to eat. We'll have lunch. I got some coupons last night.
Those. I brought something from the cafe.
Then we'll eat well. You can go to sleep till I come back.

Don't hurry.

There was no one in the lane, the small shop two blocks away, a place dark and closed, it seemed, yet he knew it was said the owner kept money in the back room behind the crowded space of counter and shelves. The faded sign boards.

              KIWI IS   BUSHELLS
                               BLUE LABEL
                                    TEA

       PEARS
FOR THE COMPLEXION
                                          LUX

Waiting till the war was ended to leave. It could have been true. A man found dead some distance down the street, no one believing he had died there. Except the police. A surprising stock on the shelves. He handed over the coupons and the man laughed. Leslie was asleep. He ran his fingers slowly across her shoulders. I have to be dreaming, she said.

The sky held a thin haze, but the streets were warm. He said: It will rain by evening.

Why do you want to go to this zoo? Are you writing something?

Not about the zoo. Not directly. I want to think.

And the animals will help.

They might.

Children had drawn squares on the broken pavement, hopping between them. Near the corner two older boys argued, one pressed back against the twisted fence.

One of those little bastards tried to make me the other day. Little sod would have fallen in and drowned if I'd said yes, he was that small. I was going to kick his arse but his mate had a knife.

Her dress was dark patterned. Like bloody camouflage,

she said. You'll lose me. Sleeveless, held about her hips. Her arms with a faint glint of colour. Rounded, well shaped, he wondered if Michael Robert might draw her. Walking in this thin light. Robert had talked about drawing from models, seemed one of the few who liked to draw from life. They think I'm still Gallery School, he said. They can't paint. I'll work from what I like.

They moved slowly along the walks of the enclosures. The animals lazy, from the warmth, or a lethargy beyond that. The cages and enclosures bare, cleaned, but somehow uncared for. Like land cleared and going back on itself. Sterile. She walked easily beside him, not talking, she might have thought he wanted to be silent. Or it might have been she did not care. A kangaroo moved slowly to the fence, and she stopped, reaching out, then halting her gesture, her arm lifted.

There used to be a lot of them around our place, he said.
What happened to them?
They got shot.
That's low, she said. I think that's really low.
They broke the fences and got into the wheat.
What were they supposed to do.
Stay on the other side. The old man did have the bank manager on his back about the crop.
Did you shoot them?
No.
Not at all?
Not at all.
Do you think we could feed this one?
We haven't got anything to feed it with.
Get something?
I don't think it wants food.
They walked on past a collection of animals that seemed to be asleep. Heads turned towards the wall of a shed. What are they? she said. Deer, I suppose. Of some kind. It's odd, but when I was a kid I cried when the old

man brought the kangaroo carcases in. He fed them to the dogs. And the pigs. I was supposed to help cut them up. Some families made soup from them. My father was angry. It made him more angry than anything I ever remember. Worried, I think. It looked like I was some kind of ring in.

He could have been right.

Yes.

No. She held him suddenly. I like you. But I don't know we're much use to each other. Have you seen enough of this?

I think so.

As they walked towards the tram she said: Did it work out?

I'll know in the morning.

When you do your writing. We could have a drink on the way back. The Swan. Did they have any swans in the zoo?

I didn't see any. There must be. Do you want to go back?

Once is enough. At least I've been.

The shelves wall this place in. An open space of tables. No one would look here. A Terra Incognito, with its own dim sky, its islands of shadow. Shores I have hardly touched. You can blame the map on the page in front of me for this, I didn't realise Dampier had travelled so far. That he had observed so acutely, written so well. Dampier turned his back on it all, the pity is all those others we celebrate did not do the same. There might have been something saved. I read here without any pattern, find my own way, haphazard. Rusden the three volumes of his *History of Australia*. John

Dunmore Lang, *An Historical And Statistical Account of New South Wales*, the title no warning of its writer's opinions. *Freedom And Independence For The Golden Lands Of Australia*, a title enough in itself. Coghlan's *Labor And Industry In Australia*. Westgarth. There is pleasure in the titles themselves, they are the books I waited for. They are all here. William Kelly looking at the Victorian goldfields, its vital, corrupt, deadly life, ground to be ripped apart and robbed, it was easier to rob one's fellows. And a lot fairer. No novel can approach his book. And Cunningham, the early years of New South Wales. *The young girls are of a mild-tempered, modest disposition, possessing much simplicity of character; and like all children of nature, credulous, and easily led into error.* In this blacked out city, the dark streets, the dance places. His accounts of the natives walking those early streets, mimics, reproducing the madness about them. *The consequential swagger of some of these dingy dandies, as they pace lordly up our streets ... no Bond-Street exquisite could ape the great man better.* A mastery of Billingsgate slang, *no white need think of competing with them in abuse or hard swearing.* Cheated by the small convict settlers, paid for the fish they brought for the settlement in old clothes, bread, and rum. Cunningham, we have need of you.

    I'm sorry to send you lists of books. But we need to talk about them and there is an excitement in these books I have to share. Sometimes when I go out and stand at the top of these steps I look at the streets and I don't believe it. But there are other things I have to look for, or look out for, I suppose, so I come to earth with reasonable speed.

    There are unexpected books, American, a book

that blends camera and words, photographs of plain exteriors, often harsh, board houses with textures that remind me of your painting. It startled me, as if you had been aware of some current, a vision, that was obscured for me. The words themselves with intricate patterns, rich, sensuous. Wright Morris. Photos of places people have made, words that lie opposite the photographs as the page opens. The introduction suggests you have someone read the text while you look at the picture. And not to compare it with cinema — memories of Fitzpatrick travel talks. I can imagine you reading, without that seeming too fanciful. The words are the rhythms and intonations of folk speech. There is one photo of a wooden street shack, with very strong contrasts of light and shadow — very dark shadow. The prose is headed *Martha Lee*.

> Shadows are the way things lay-me-down. Papa can lay-me-down across the road. Mr Clarke's store can lay-me-down on the barn and the barn can lay-me-down on Mr Clarke. Everything that stands up must lay-me-down. The fence, trucks in the road, birds that fly low, poles, things, myself. I can lay-me-down clear to the door. Everything tall as smooth as everything short. Everything loud as quiet as everything still. Even birds know why it is and don't sing. Even the night must come and lay-me-down to sleep.

> Not in this city. And I'm not saying you can rush out into the middle of Swanston Street and write that. But how beautiful. And where are the contemporary words for this city? This country? Words. The painters have their images, there are no words to compete with them in what they are

doing. A few, a very few, of the poets come closest. It's as if I've made a wrong choice. Yet no choice at all.

He heard her footsteps on the path, then the pause while she looked in her handbag for the key. She never took it out of her bag until she was at the door. If I drop the thing on this path, she said, it's gone. Down with a lot of other shit I wouldn't be surprised. He hesitated near the door to the lane, but she was inside, closing the door quietly. He said: I didn't expect you so early.

It was slack. He said I might as well go. Had something on out the back, I'd say. And I was tired.

I was going out.

Oh. Yes, I see.

She sat on the bed, taking off her shoes, her movements quick, impatient, but the shoes dropping neatly together. He said: Why?

Why what?

Did you want to do something?

Not if you're going out.

I didn't think you'd be in for a couple of hours.

Well I am. And I'm that bloody bored. Tired of it. The lot.

I'm sorry.

Have you been working?

Writing. I'll make you a cup of tea.

Please. Yes. She swung her legs onto the bed, lay back, straight, still. You take that seriously, don't you.

Making you tea?

You'd better. Writing.

Yes.

Do you, you know, get it published?

Not much. Two stories just recently. In a new magazine that's the best hope for any writing that's not the same as everything else has always been. *Angry Penguins.*

It's strange, she said.

Strange?

The things you're worried about.

Like writing?

That. Yes.

Why?

I don't know, she said. I'm glad about the stories. But it all loses me.

It loses me. And there's all the bloody censorship. Ridiculous. I had a character pissed on a wall in a lane.

Like outside.

Yes. Like outside. The printers wouldn't set it.

So he held it.

He had to. It's hard to know what you can get into writing. Or why we are so afraid. It goes all the way from official trouble at one end, holding up licences, newsprint, threats, to righteous bloody printers at the other.

So, she said, it's all shit. It really is. The lot.

It'll break. It has to. And there are people trying. The Reeds. I've met them. Max Harris. But it's not easy. And there are new magazines. Do you want to go out?

I might.

I was going to see a painter. Michael Robert. He told me how to get there, but you can get lost out around that part.

Not my line.

It doesn't have to be. If you're wanting a change. From here.

Yes, she said. From here. Like this? I can't be bothered getting dressed.

Like you are.

We can go out the back way. I think the old bastard's in the front room. Must be money counting night.

Beyond the station, the streets were empty. You didn't say it was so far, she said.

I didn't know it was so far. It's not, if we hadn't gone down the wrong street.

I wouldn't live out here.

He's had this place a while, I think. Somewhere to live.

Somewhere to paint, she said.

Robert opened the door of a house that fronted the pavement, a door painted white, faded. A passageway divided the house. This side, he said. We've got the cracked wall. I put a mural over it. The room had closed windows to the street, a table crowded with bottles, jars, paints, two pieces of a cracked marble washstand-top streaked with ridges and craters of colours. Two chairs, some cushions on the floor. For all its clutter, organised, almost tidy. A sense of order, and lack of space very different from the sprawl of Jackson's place. He saw Leslie look about the room, as if without curiosity, casual, contained. Sitting on the cushions a woman, staring at them, long dark hair, a deeper colour he thought, black, brushed smooth. Looking at them carefully, an antagonism clear enough. Wide dark eyes, aware, hard. Eve Lest. A writer, it was said, though he had never seen any of her work. Some, unpublished, passed about among friends, and he had not seen that, either. Said to have been, to be, he did not know, married to Robert. Michael has been around for a long time, Jackson said. She lives with him. He survives. Maybe she helps him. Somehow. She won't like you. But you'll have to take it. A sleek, smooth face, small features, dead but for the contempt of the eyes. Robert moved one of the chairs for Leslie. She did not look at the other woman.

Robert had completed a series of night scenes of city streets, corners, trams and cars against dark buildings, figures in sudden slashes of light. Faces, bodies in sharp colour, emphasis, against the heavy backgrounds. How to feel bad and look worse, Leslie said suddenly. I know.

Robert paused, his hand on one of the paintings. Honesty, he said. There's not that much of it about here. Leslie, can I make some sketches. Your face. Looking like that. Held forward. Like you were.

I thought she was asleep, Eve said.

Well, I was.

Keep looking at the paintings. Sorry about them. He worked quickly. Eve got up from the cushions, walked about the room. That's no good, Michael. You're not getting anything.

What I need. Leslie's face is interesting.

It's been called a few things, the girl said. And no one meant that.

Quite, Eve said.

Perhaps we could have some tea, Eve. I had some wine last week. Some of Eve's friends arrived. So it's tea. There is some tea?

I don't need tea. You can make them some.

He supposed Leslie would refuse, and they would go. But she was amused, moved her head, faced into the light from the lamp, away, as Robert asked, and when he finished he went down the passage to make the tea. Eve left the room. He said: Do you like the paintings?

Like them? Of course not. But he's clever.

Very. But for all that's in them, somehow dead. I don't think he meant that. It's strange. I mean, compare them with Jackson's.

If you were like that why not be dead. Will he make me look like them?

Robert brought a tray, and cups. No biscuits, he said. This place. We'll starve here.

In the street Leslie said: He's a nice guy. He's got problems with the girl friend.

She was a bit on edge. Not someone you'd like. Robert works in an industrial design place. They called him up, but he was B2 or something, farting about in some office boy job, and the firm he'd worked for got a defence contract, and got him out. I think the lady was going to take off at that time. Probably with someone else. Apparently can't stand being left alone.

Those faces he paints. He'd better not make me that way. I liked him. But her hair. Do you reckon he paints it over once a week?

Unkind. Actually I'd say it was for real.

It was a good idea going there, she said. I feel better.

In the late afternoon he took the tram to Bourke Street, walking the crowded pavements to the gallery. The number of civilians in the streets still surprised him, reminder of the almost bare streets of the city he had left, the older men, women, and children, a city denuded.

He went into the gallery with less expectation, a sense that something of the urgency and vitality must have faded. Less surprise, now, but the crowded walls still spoke in a way he could not have imagined. These paintings would be dispersed, but there would be others, all this would go on. You were wrong, Barbara, he said, and could not be sure he had not spoken. A man affected by what many regarded as a kind of madness. A contagion. He moved slowly along the walls that opened out to other walls, streets, patches of barren countryside, as they opened to issues he knew he could only partly encompass. I try to find words, he said. And there are no words. These are the images for this time, and words are wrong. He stood by the three figures of war, each time he came he was drawn back to this. Tucker. *Vicissitudes Of War*. Less dramatic, in some ways, than *The Bombing*. But when you let all the words fall, he said, beyond the words of style, of method and philosophy, these three figures spoke. With a terrible despair. And irony. Alone. Speaking to no one in their gas green world devoid of all

landmark. They existed. They were.
   You were lost.
   Yes, he said.
   I know. George Edmonds laughed. Yes.
   And afraid.
   You must come out and see us again one evening.
   Eve Lest stood behind Edmonds. He had not seen her. Her dark eyes on him. Dismissing him. Eyes like some in these paintings, along these walls. He saw it now. The sense of gloss, the hardness of surface, the sense of desolation. She moved Edmonds away. Edmonds half turning to say: Ring us and we can arrange something.

   The painting had been turned to the wall. She was sitting at the table, cold meat and potato on a plate pushed aside, he thought she had been asleep. He said: I forgot about the painting.
   I don't want to eat this. I brought it from the cafe. Do you want it?
   If you don't. Yes.
   Make some tea and it's all yours.
   She drank the hot tea quickly. She said: I think there's a bit of a problem. The old bastard has been acting very strange. Something's got to him. He says they've been asking him if he's letting rooms here.
   He could say no to that and be telling the truth.
   But he's got jumpy.
   Who was asking him?
   He said the Council. I don't think he was telling the truth. You can't tell with him.
   But someone was asking.
   I'd say so. He's worried.
   Our fearless feds, the secret police.

Don't joke about that. I hope not. I don't need those bastards.

They're that stupid they wouldn't know. But it doesn't have to be them. Unless he's in something else.

It doesn't want to be.

The meat is quite good. The last piece. Sure?

I'm not hungry.

You said he had a couple of other places.

He does. Falling down. He looks for property for after the war.

It depends where the places are. There's some odd characters moved into the rent racket it seems. According to Harry. Who'd probably like to graduate to that himself. It could just be enquiries.

Rub my back, she said. Please. I'm tired. Bloody tired.

She slipped off the thin dress, unhooked her bra, lay face down on the bed, her arms along her sides. Her back firm, his fingers drawing over her shoulders, down, the skin colouring, fading. I don't think it could be that, she said. That wouldn't involve me. No, he's that cagey he never says anything straight out. But he's trying to say something. It could be he wants to get me out.

You think I should go.

I think it might be best. Look, I've never asked you anything. I don't want to know. But it might be you.

It might be. I'm not sure anything like that would be likely. I wouldn't involve you in anything, Leslie.

It's just I've had problems. I don't want any more of that.

I can ask and see if there's anything around.

I don't want to be involved. I don't want you to go. You believe that?

Yes, he said. And I've liked it here. With you.

I don't know why.

Why not?

Well, why not. I'm sorry about it. Just for a time, and we

can see. He is trying to say something.

A waiting room. Neither of them had ever had possessions that he had seen, clothes, little else. They had not brought anything over here. A few photos of Harry in the ring, one a good press photo of a punch that won him a six round bout. He had to go down then, Harry said. Before I fell down. A posed photograph, trunks and gloves, his hair cleanly parted, a high left hand. He remembered those. The lack of possessions an achievement. A statement. On the mantel, over the half closed fireplace where someone had burned papers, French had placed dolls, one on a long stick, a small brown and black monkey, a large animal, a bear, two clowns' heads, chocolate boxes. Trophies, she said. Sideshows. Stalls. He keeps winning them. My right hand, Harry said. The bedroom behind this room no different, the cubicle that was a kitchen clean but untidy. He knew French's disregard of housework. Harry said: I don't think it's anything.

But she is worried, he said.

Leslie worries. Not often. You go with it. If there was something it's most likely some of the mob in the rents. No one knows what will happen after the war, but they can't keep on with tenancy rights. Houses could be something big. They're getting edgy.

I'll have to move.

Sleep here tonight. It's late anyhow. We've only got the one bed and with French in that no one else gets much.

Sleep on the other side of me, French said. He won't know.

Tomorrow you can get a bed down the road a bit. It's a rat hole, but there's a place further out might do. Burwood way. Would you go out there?

I don't know where it is, he said. But yes.

I think Leslie's panicked on this. I don't see the hurry. But that's Leslie. She'll probably forget it in a week or so. I can get onto this other character. His old man has it rented. A sort of lollywater specialist. Stays in this one room most of the time. Drinks this stuff. The room's full of empty bottles. Billy's the one to see. He's got a woman there and a kid. He drives a truck. Quite funny, because he goes through on anything. But the army don't want him, I mean he could get at the canteen, and drivers are hard to come by around town.

Sounds ideal.

It's all Harry, French said.

He has this room, all right for a couple, but he doesn't want that. They can be hard to get out.

I'll make coffee, French said. But it gets worse all the time. There's some American around, but we can't get it.

Problem, Harry said. And the grog's short. A matter of time. All things possible. Do you want some work?

Doing what?

Supplying.

But what?

There's some hard stuff coming in. If I could get onto that.

Would you put that around?

Why not?

It's fairly drastic. Isn't it?

It can be. What they do with it isn't my worry. They'll find something to bugger themselves with if they can't get that.

Maybe not as rough as that.

There are enough poor bastards around here rotten with grog, metho, you name it. It's not the stuff, it's the people. You can't make them take it. Or any other bloody thing. They want to. Okay.

They wouldn't have the money. For this stuff. Not round here.

No. It goes higher up. But no difference. It's what they want.

I'd rather not, Harry.

No worry then. And it can get hard. You get people looking for you if they can't get it regular. The mob I work for, they wouldn't like it at all if I'm in that. Not if I was on my own.

You're bloody mad, Harry, French said. It's all right now, why mess about.

It's sitting there. Like those monkeys. Chocolates. Someone has to knock it off. But the petrol coupons have come good. You can do that?

I can do that.

They washed the glasses and cups, French brought a rug, she stood close to him by the narrow couch, lifted her hand slowly and touched his face.

All we've got. And don't worry about what Harry says.

He stood by the window, the street dark. Near the opposite fence shadows moved. A dog. Cats. They were too late. A street abandoned. Ruins for some explorer to stumble on. He lay on the couch, pulled the rug carefully round him. A cold from the street. From the walls. The building with its own sounds, unfamiliar. Leslie in her own bed. Alone. Perhaps.

The woman was elderly, thin, a plain dress, a cardigan buttoned tightly, and slippers. She held the door half open.

It's three sharing, she said. Only a bed like. If you want that.

For a few days.

I'll show you.

The passage cut through the house, open onto a lean-to verandah, a narrow space of yard. The small sentry box lavatory. Clear from the front door. The clean brown boards of the passage, a thin central strip of lino. The room with three beds, a wardrobe, small table. The window curtained, beyond it the street. Step from window to pavement. They might have come and gone that way. The smell of cigarette smoke.

Yes, he said. For a few days.

In advance. A week?

If you want that.

It's like they don't come back. Sometimes. She smiled suddenly, without teeth, her face wrinkling.

I understand, he said.

You can leave them here, Jackson said. There's that much rubbish no one will notice.

The books made a pile on the floor by the paintings. I'm going into town, Jackson said. We could have a drink. I've got to see Reg Dover first. Some things he's just finished.

The paintings were carefully arranged about the back room. The single window to the square of back yard gave a clear light. The rooms clean, cared for, the big woman stood in the doorway, watching them. Outside he could hear the two children. Machines, long work spaces, heavy machinery, figures bent, entwined about the metal. Some under light, harsh, the edges of spaces dark, some outside in work yards, heavy grey clouds holding like the walls of the buildings. The figures held. Good, Jackson said. Not for me, not altogether, but it's right this time.

It doesn't have to be for you, Dover said.

They'll have to look at these.

Why aren't they for you?

Nothing to do with it. You make a statement with this. I'd make one a bit different.

There was a coke fire in the front room. Dover stayed near it. He seemed to shiver, a kind of trembling when he was away from the warmth. The woman poured them tea, offered the plain biscuits. The two young girls came to the door. She said: He's been working too much lately.

Painting? Jackson said.

Yes. And a lot of overtime at work.

So don't go on about it, Dover said.

I never see him.

Best way, Jackson said. Painters are not for seeing. He's going well, Jane. Tell him to give up work.

You tell him, Jane said.

In the street Jackson kicked carefully at an empty tin. He does work too hard. He's in a factory. Defence work. He's wound up about the war. Tried to enlist but they kept him out.

The paintings are good. A bit, what, stylised? Propaganda?

What I nearly said, then got away from it.

But good.

Yes. He's sold some of his earlier stuff. He could some of this. What he says, how he says it, people will take. Do you want a drink?

I'll pass up the drink, he said. It's getting late.

You can go back to my place. Keep you away from that room.

The small room. A faint light from the closed window. The man coming in late, stripping his trousers, socks. His shoes under the bed. To pull back the sheet, blanket. Before long to breathe heavily, a curious soft sound, after a time like sobbing. The smell of cigarettes. The bloody room, he said. I'll look for a film. There's a rather odd girl I know.

Jackson raised his hand. I thought you had one of them.

As they came out onto the street she said: Did you like the film?

In a way. Quite well made.

It was sad.

Life in those coal valleys. Yes. It never was green, however he thought of it.

Do we have places like that?

Oh yes.

I don't want to think about it. And the news reel

frightened me.
   A bad night. I'm sorry, Jessica.
   No. I didn't mean that.
   And I wouldn't worry too much about the news reels. One day we might know how much of them was ever true.
   But they are real.
   How would we know. And what would we do if they weren't.
   Let's have coffee, she said.

It was early, few tables taken in the cafe. Two men by the painted-over window, an old man, alone, near the door. Leslie said: It doesn't seem too good.
   It'll do.
   I'm sorry about it. I am.
   It's not your fault.
   Maybe we should have waited. But he was out the back this morning when I left. And he never comes out.
   Could be a call of nature. Delayed.
   He'd never let anything like that go.
   I may have another place by the end of the week. Will you come out and have a look at it?
   I might. Look, have the lunch. Not bad today. I'll get you something.
   When she stood by the table she said: Is Harry fixing this other place?
   I wouldn't even know where it was.
   I worry a bit about him.
   A few people have worried about Harry. Some got counted out.
   Did he ever fight under another name?
   When he started he had some kind of fancy name. But I think he dropped that very early. Why?
   Something French said. I don't think she realised. Then he came in and I forgot.
   A lot of them use another name.

155

I don't see how he fits into what he's doing. The mob he's with.

I'd say it goes a long way back.

It doesn't matter. He's very sure of himself.

In a way. Not something I'd bet on. But he gets by.

He does that. But you should be careful. Do you like the salad?

It's very good. You can't get salad, most places.

She leaned towards him, her breath sharp, onion, she picked a small piece from the plate, bit quickly. Lui thinks I'm your woman. So you get a good deal.

I'm glad of that. But you're your own woman, Leslie.

Tonight. We can see if there's anything.

The house had its own silence. Early, Billy left for work, there were voices, the woman's loud, often angry, the crying of the child. He saw her about the house, thin, tense, a face sharp, angular, fair hair elaborately waved. In the early mornings wearing a gown over a short nightdress, her bare legs thin and white. Somewhere about mid morning, carefully dressed, her hair immaculate in its ridges and waves, she went out, taking the child in an expensive looking pusher, slamming the front door that would not catch. She left the back of the house open, the slam of the front door may have been to annoy the old man in the front room. Perhaps to wake him. She walked down the street as if to put the place behind her for good. About four she returned, and from the noise in the kitchen, her step in the passage, without much sense of welcome. Little sound, when she was gone, from the other front room. A cough, the day's paper dropped on the floor. It was brought every morning, Billy threw it in to his father, onto the bed, before he left. A room with little furniture, he went in to pay the rent, the old double bed, its head against one wall, the same wall shaken by the front door in its savage closing, the bed reaching out dead centre of the room, a fireplace backing that in the adjoining room. A tall, dark wardrobe, a dressing table. The room not dirty, somehow, but holding dust. The floor, the dressing table, a faint patina. In the fireplace the empty cool drink bottles. At times spreading out across the hearth as if in the darkness they multiplied. The fireplace shadowed, but towards the edge of the standing bottles some appeared unopened. They gave a greenish light to the dark hearth and the cave of the fireplace.

Once a week the old man, dressed in a dark grey suit, and dark felt hat, locked his door and went down the street. In the early afternoon. It might have been a betting foray. Never carrying anything that could be seen when he left, or came back. The rest of the time he perhaps lay on the wide bed. With the paper.

The house, reminding him sharply of the house at the farm, took on the sounds of timber that seemed to shift, expand, crack with the heat, echo the slow rasp of boughs in the wind that swept the long street. In between, the quiet. He listened as he worked in the morning, or read.

A good room to paint in, Jackson said. Space. Light. Take mess. If that's what you want. I had to do without anything decent for long enough. A bit far out for me or we might share.

Too far from your houses and streets. Though you might find a few not far from here. You'll never leave. But what will you do when they pull all those houses of yours down?

That day won't come.

They'll clear those areas. Afterwards.

After what. No. If they did they'd only make something worse.

They cooked a meal in the evening, among the few things in the makeshift kitchen at the back.

Was this the washhouse? Jackson said.

There's one of those out the back. But you can't get into

it. The door's jammed or locked.
Are you writing?
A great deal.
Good?
I doubt it.
Then you're all right. If a thing is bad enough they'll read it.
I'm glad about that. Thanks.
You can put a couple of paintings in this room. With the one your girlfriend wouldn't look at. No other bugger wants them. They'll fill it up for you.
He set one of the paintings over the fireplace, on the mantel. The others stood near the window.
Why don't you hang them, Jessica said.
The wall. My castle might come down.
They look quite well in here.
There's too much light. But at night, in the light from that one globe up there they come to life. The colours live. They are night pieces.
She had not seen them at night. She did not come often, a Saturday or Sunday afternoon. You're afraid of the place, he said. But she said: No. Of course not. When she did come they were in the room only briefly, he showed her the walk down the old railway cutting, or out towards Balwyn, the older houses and gardens, streets shaded with trees.
Later, she said, you must see the street trees at Toorak. Everywhere in flower. The gardens. Some wonderful old houses. I'll show you.
She would never stay for a meal, a single cup of tea at most, repelled perhaps by the kitchen at the back. Which she could have seen only at the end of the passage. The dishes are clean, he said. The cups. Quite okay.
Her face suddenly white, he thought she might cry, at times she seemed easily close to tears. It's all right, he said. I didn't mean anything.

Her own curiosity bringing her. Standing just inside the door, to look about the room with a grave attention. As if she must understand it. It's a bit spare, he said. Quiet. Peaceful in a way.

Where you work.

Where I live.

Is what you are doing, your writing, I mean, going well?

I don't know, he said. Some short things I think are all right. I seem to be able to shape them to what I want. But I'm trying to do something much longer and I don't know. I want a realism, yes. But more than that. I can see what I want in some of the work the painters are doing now. But I don't know that I can get it.

If I was any sort of a reader, she said, I could look at it and perhaps help.

No one can help.

She looked quickly away, and he said: It's not personal. I appreciate what you say. It's a kind of private battle.

The room had its own door to the front verandah. You won't have to see anyone, he said. You wouldn't come if you had to go through the house, would you. See people.

She looked at the old casement windows, the neglected strip of garden between the house and front fence. I don't know. Do you mind?

Another window opened close to the side fence. Beyond the fence a vacant block and an old brick house, screened by shrubs, where he had seen no one, nothing moved. The floor of the room sloped from the fireplace, movement of the floor stumps had cracked one wall, painted over, the crack reappearing in a long crooked scar, and he was reminded of Michael Robert's solution to his own wall. There was a deep wicker chair, a lounge of the same sort, furniture he could not remember seeing anywhere else, worn so that they moved in a kind of spread, not uncomfortable. In the middle of the room a round, once polished, table, in its exact centre a cross or old fashioned

X burnt. One straightbacked chair at the table, the double bed near the side window, blankets and a quilt, no sheets. The bed provided fleas, retreating slowly to insecticide powder. But comfortable, in the early mornings the thin boughs along the fence patterned against the light. They won't bother you, Harry said. Watch out for Billy. Not that you'll see him much. But don't leave money about. Don't leave it. Put it under your pillow at night. He can't help it. It'll go. I feel sorry for him. The ds are waiting for something to go where he works and they'll take him for it. The poor bastard's got no chance. But he's shrewd.

The room quiet. The street cut off by the railway line, a branch line little used. He had not seen a car in the street. Mid morning a few women left the houses to shop. Earlier, men took the short cut across the line to the station. He worked at the round table which he left in the centre of the room, at night the single globe directly above it. But I don't know how long I can keep it, he said. I'll run out of money. Harry said: I can get you something. Places they won't stop you at. There's room for someone doing a round. The two men at the shop, the older cheerful, smiling. The younger man not speaking. Looking at them only once. That bugger might get a bit towey, Harry said. Have to sort him out. No, he said, not if it's collecting. No. Something else, I'll have to do it. Mornings when he was tired of the room, he could walk down to the old railway line, through the heavy clay cuttings, to the flats by the river. There were trees, a thin undergrowth along the banks. He lay in the shade and watched the still clear water. Dragon flies or wasps dipped at the surface. A silence. The silence of the days they walked along the beach, the sand clear, washed, thin strips of weed at the tide mark. Carrying almost nothing to eat or drink. Stripping their clothes to swim. Behind the dunes, sheltered from the wind, the sand spreading about the thick wattles. The heat and the heavy shade.

I'll catch the tram, he said.

The lane two blocks up past the markets, Harry said. Don't be late. I don't want to hang about there.

The car backed down the narrow way that was blocked by a yard stacked with old building material. Someone had been at the stacks. Or they had collapsed. The rats growing too big. Heavy shadow from the buildings in the early dark made the car hard to see. There seemed no one in it. A mid thirties V8, hard, heavy, black. A light rain filmed the metal, the dust. It would be locked. Then he saw Harry lying on the seat. If he was asleep. Finished his collecting early. And he would not have wanted to stay here. He tapped on the glass. The door was not locked. In the darkness he was not sure. But the blood had run across the clothes, the shirt and coat. Over the seats onto the floor mat. An odd thin stain. The lane was empty. He lifted the coat. The wallet and papers in the inside pocket. They were clear and free of blood. In the left lower pocket the keys. He opened the rear door, the floor mat was even, untouched. He took out the thin cloth bag. There was a light now in the upper floor of one building. He looked at the front seat, he reached in and for a moment touched the upthrust shoulder, his fingers gripping, closed the doors. The shadow was heavy down the side of the lane.

The line of houses along the street might all have been built the same. Altered only by time and tenants. The corner building two storeyed, once a shop. Closed now, but lived in. A warren, he said, and Harry laughed. That's what it's bloody for. You come and go. No one sees. There was a light behind the curtains, he slid Harry's key into the lock. In the kitchen the table was set. French said: You. I thought it was Harry.

He said: I used his keys. Something's happened. It's not good.

Her hand touched the table. I knew, she said. I knew it would.

I'm sorry to have to be like this.

What is it?

He was in the car.

You can tell me, she said.

It was a knife. I'd say just once. But nothing was touched. Everything was there. It doesn't make sense.

It makes sense.

It might have been some stupid bloody argument. Something he said. Some of those sods up there get very touchy. I mean about things that don't matter.

Because, she said, there's bugger all they can do about what does matter.

If you like. But it seems wrong. Nothing taken.

Unless they were afraid.

It might be that.

I mean, Harry was one thing. Messing about with the mob he worked for was something else.

It had to be someone he knew. Didn't expect.

She moved away from the table. Her hands twisted quickly, as if she would touch him. She said: I'm sorry. For him. He was good to me. More than anyone. But he took risks. I told him.

I had to see you before I did anything.

There's nothing to do. It would start too much.

Yes, he said. But you're sure?

Oh yes.

There was this, he said. He put the bag on the table.

Open it, she said.

He placed the notes across the table. You should have this French. There's a lot there. But put it away somewhere. They'll look for it. Later it should be all right.

They will look. But I can't take it.

You'll have to.

You needn't have come back here. I wouldn't have

known. I won't take it all.

What I'd like to do, he said, is keep the ID card. The exemption.

We have to make sense of this, she said. Yes. And the ration cards. I can always get those. Keep the papers. We'd only have to destroy them. Half the money.

No.

Some.

Some if you are sure.

Of course. I'll wait and see what happens. They'll come here. But there's nothing for them.

Me, if I'm still here.

He wouldn't have gone in till tomorrow. About twelve. Tonight is all right. Do you want to eat?

I don't think so.

A drink.

That. Yes.

I knew it would happen. Something.

I couldn't leave the money. It wouldn't stay there. Whoever finds it. If the police found it, they're not stupid enough to put it all on a station table. Not that kind of money. And they won't want to know about what happened.

They won't want to know, she said. It's not them worry me, as long as there's nothing to bring them here. And you've stopped that. What will you do?

Nothing. I don't know anything. Like them.

With those papers, it could be trouble.

They're not in his name. He only wanted them for something going wrong. Confuse things. I'd only need them that way.

If I can help.

If I can help you. I'm sorry, French.

Good luck, she said. Not there's that much of it about.

The cup was delicately patterned, a thin line of deep green about the rim, the outer edge of the handle, fine green tendrils and leaves, a few flowers, a single tendril and flower on the inner surface near the rim. Kathy said: It is quite beautiful. This cup.
   It's not exactly new. You have never looked at it.
   Perhaps. You've always liked china.
   Yes. And I didn't realise you'd noticed that, either.
   Mother, Richard and I have worked it out. I'm going to Sydney. I have to. I can't get work here. And dashing backwards and forwards doesn't help.
   We have talked about this before.
   I know that. It's not something that will go away.
   Jessica said: You mean you are leaving him.
   You put things in such a weird way.
   But you obviously are.
   All right. If you must see it that way.
   And the girls?
   They will be fine. They go to boarding school anyhow, and nothing will be that much different.
   I used to go to boarding school. I didn't like it. I used to wish I was at home.

You were fond of your house. That house. That you never took me to see.

I was never able to.

Of course you were. It doesn't matter now. You could have gone back there when you and father split up.

We didn't split up.

Oh god. Like Richard and me.

Do you think this is my fault?

No. Of course not.

I had the shop, she said. It was doing well. I would have had to give that up if I had gone home. And it would have been too hard to start again with that kind of thing in Melbourne. I didn't want to go back there. Kathy, I like clothes. I always have. Not a snob thing. Certainly you can make money out of that. Yes. Or selling rags. I like cloth. Fabric. Colours. I like designing.

You've done all that well enough. Very well. And you've always dressed beautifully. I was very proud of you when we went out when I was a child.

Not now?

Don't be ridiculous. Very much now.

Charles always dressed so well.

Mother, you're not saying that's what attracted you to him? Though it has crossed my mind to wonder what did.

Jessica moved her cup slightly, pushed it away. No. I drink too much coffee. It's supposed to be bad for you. Everything is, now. I don't know how we survived. But yes, in a way it did. Of course. He was very handsome in his uniform.

That's absurd. It's about the oldest thing in the book. A uniform. What has that to do with clothes.

He could wear them. And of course he didn't always wear uniform.

Mother, you've gone back somewhere. I don't know where you are. I suppose he was well dressed. In a formal way.

Charles was formal.

As I remember, yes.

That's unkind.

And very certain, somehow. Sure of himself. Sure he was right.

I suppose so. It might have been easier to be sure of things once.

I don't really know why the pair of you didn't get on.

I thought you might be like me, Kathy. When you were a child you loved to look at my dresses.

Wardrobes of them. Yes, I did.

You wore them. Acting. I used to watch you. But I thought you might come into the shop with me.

I would have been no use to you.

The racks of dresses. Colours and feel. The sense of them changing her. And her mother coming suddenly into her room one late afternoon as she struggled with a script. Walking past her, to stare at the shadowed garden. Do you have men? Other men now? Her mother turning from the window, not hearing. Then she said: Kathy, that's a terrible thing to say. I didn't say. I asked. You can't ask your mother things like that. You mean you won't answer things like that. The words on the paper, the voices. Her mother not looking at her. Seeing the shadows and the darkening lawn. The pair of them caught in a scene she suddenly wanted to play out. Mother, it doesn't belong to Charles for eternity. He has gone. You're beautiful. An attractive woman. You should. Jessica said: Do you want me to help you with reading that?

It's strange really, Kathy said. My children would never have been interested in my clothes. Except maybe if they wanted to grab something to wear and they were in a hurry. But there's so much made for them now. Choice everywhere. I suppose we were about the last children would have done that. Well, anyway, I did come here to tell you about Richard and me. I'll have to go now. You can go and tell Richard you disapprove. He listens to you.

Jessica closed the book. The girl said: What are you looking at?

Just a letter I had. Reminded me of something.

Who was it?

It doesn't matter. Joyce's mother, if you must know.

Kathy picked up the album. She turned a few of the pages. You've been looking at photos of that house. I don't know why you didn't live there. I think I hate that place. I don't think you should sit there dreaming.

Why shouldn't I. Just because you're not a dreamer, Kathy.

Oh I have a few. But you should have lived in that place. You and father could have raised some quite different family on the country estate.

I could have had the house, I think, when mother died. But I'm quite sure Charles would have sold it. He needed capital then.

He couldn't have done that.

He probably could have.

You could have stopped him.

Not so easy, Kathy. Not in those days. No, he'd have had his way and I couldn't see it go like that. At least my cousins want to live in it. As long as they can. Those places have become dreadfully expensive to keep up.

I somehow never thought of the two of you involved like that. But I suppose you could have been. I mean, surely he was always very considerate.

Oh, very considerate. And very ruthless.

My father?

Charles. He spent all those first years after the war making money. Security.

As I hear it, mother, so did everyone else.

He did it very well. He didn't have much money. People thought he did. But he had his way. A kind of instinct. Perhaps why he was such a good fighter pilot in the war.

That's a bit far fetched, isn't it?

He was ruthless. He would pursue things.

I don't really know very much about him, do I. I suppose I haven't wanted to. He certainly didn't want to know about us.

Kathy, I don't think you understand anything about that time.

Maybe not. I'm not one for wars.

It was why he came over here. He thought this place was the end of the earth. But someone he knew in the services lived in Perth and offered him a partnership. It was a good opening.

In real estate. Well, I did hear enough about that.

Partly. They never actually put it about, but they had a couple of used car businesses. Very profitable then. Later, new car agencies. Of course, when he could he went back to Melbourne.

He did indeed. How about the partner? Did I ever know him?

Not really. Charles somehow took over from him. I don't know what happened to him.

You're not saying he fell out of the sky?

I don't think that's very funny.

The partner probably didn't either.

You don't know anything about it.

And he left you.

Darling, I didn't want to go.

He left us.

Kathy, you shouldn't be too hard about these kind of things.

I don't care, she said. I did at first. I don't care at all. Not now.

She looked at the letter and the album on the table. It's always these sort of things, she said. It frightens me. Can't we go out. Anywhere. Please.

The balcony gave a view of the street, the lines of trees in heavy leaf. Some older houses, one white painted, weatherboard, held in shrubs, beside it a new place, glass, round towered. Two dogs on the lawn opposite. Trees shaded the balcony.

You should come and see us more often, Maria said. It's not as if we were so far away.

I don't think James thinks that, he said.

He comes to talk to me about a book he says is different, James said. That chills me.

You need a book that is different, Maria said. All those glossies. You really do. You should listen to him.

The iron furniture painted white. The comfortable cushions. She was taller than her husband. The strongly patterned sun dress, her fine brown skin, back and arms, long black hair held at her neck. A red ribbon. It should all have been too much. Something to write about, but he never had.

I do listen, James said. He told me he had a book that was different. Perhaps original. A plan to put me into liquidation.

No one has quite managed that yet, she said. Though there might come a time it should happen.

You should go and live with him. There might come a time when that should happen.

There might, James. Yes.

If you've finished deciding my future, he said. Maria would never live with me. Both of you have far too much sense. What I tried to tell James, I wanted to do a book on the destruction of Australia.

He thought he might call it the death of a country.

It sounds fine, Maria said.

It goes back a long way. What I suspected a long time ago. But I think I fought against believing it. It was this sense that we have a strong hatred of this country. Hidden under all the right sentiments of course.

Hidden under some of James' delectable glossies.

I didn't think it was so obvious then. In fact I don't think it was. Now, we're desperately uncomfortable with it. And we can only rest when we've stripped its trees, destroyed its soil, killed its animals. I'm sorry, it's your wonderful coffee, Maria. I like coming here.

But you won't come more often.

That would spoil it.

Another destruction, James said. He is better at home with his novels.

I'm afraid of words now, he said. Or I think so. They need help. And I don't expect a generation, two generations, I suppose, raised on television, to accept any view of things that isn't going to come right in the next instalment. Or at worst the one after.

He's quite right, Maria said. You should do this book.

He wants it in black and white. Big photographs. Terse text.

I remember a book by Wright Morris, he said. I saw it in the early forties, I think. I've always remembered. Something like that, but not his sense of belief in people.

You could have a lot of beliefs at that time, James said. I'm always coming across them.

There would be people in this book? Maria said.

No. Only where they've been.

The faint pattern of leaf shadow moved over the china, the white tray and the cloth. Maria said: You could carry one book like that.

We could distribute it to schools, James said. They

could cut it up for classroom montage.

I will go and live with him, Maria said. Or maybe we will both go and live in Greece.

I'm glad you could come, Kathy said. I don't know why you don't come over here more often.

I don't think I really like moving about. And the shops can't be left for long.

Long enough for you to enjoy yourself.

Perhaps. She stepped across to the window, looking down into the street. The neat terrace houses, renovated, some with brick walls to the pavement, creepers, shrubs. Some without concealment. Cars parked along the street. She said: It is very pleasant here, Kathy.

It is very pleasant. We are lucky to have it. All becoming quite crazily expensive. Helen had some money, I had my usual bugger all but Richard provided. He really is very good.

I'm fond of Richard. I just wish you two weren't so, oh, I don't know. It's you, isn't it. You won't go back to him.

You can't go back to people, mother. As it is, we have some kind of respect for each other. A sort of friendship. Why destroy that. I have to live here.

So it seems. Sydney the centre of all things. Sometimes it reminds me of Rome in the days of the empire.

You have a point.

The centre of your kind of things, anyhow.

Right. I'm glad you came on up here.

I had to see some people in Melbourne. Supply mixups. I'm very glad I'm not trying to run my business there. Some things I hear are quite frightening.

A great place for gangs and standover men. Sweated labour. Good plots. But they say it always was. Sydney of course simply assumes corruption, it's just life. You didn't go up to the old property?

No. I came on up here.

Good. I'll have to rush, but we'll have lunch. About one. Have a drink if I'm late.

The terrace. The water. The bridge beyond. A tourist brochure. A local tv drama. Kathy sitting at a table like this. Not a city she liked, their own quiet river was more pleasant. Tranquil. Despite everything. Their strange need to encroach on the water. As if it were a reproach. Oh god, yes, she said. I will have something to drink, please. Closed restaurants north of the city, in old buildings. Windowless. Northbridge. Darkness was all. I hate darkness, she said. Perhaps they did do it better here. Kathy was not late, coming along the terrace, walking quickly, speaking to someone at another table.

I'm not late, she said. It's a beautiful day.

If it doesn't rain in the afternoon, Jessica said.

You judge everything by that terrible desert. The rain keeps us fresh and clean here.

She sat at the table, smiling at the waiter, who knew her. At home. At ease. As if this was her place. Yes, Jessica said. I suppose it is, of course.

I'm sorry?

Nothing Kathy. Are you busy?

I've been keeping a surprise for you. It was only definite this morning. I'm going to be in a play by your favourite author.

Do I have one?

You seem to have read all his books.

Oh. I see. I suppose I did.

You got them from the library. Even when they were about all you did get. A few on the shelf. Before you gave up for tv.

It's true I don't read very much.

You read his books. I used to wonder. I didn't much like

them. Her mother saying you are very restless. And you are certainly well enough to go to school tomorrow. It's very boring being at home she said. I'm tired of it. Her mother looking at the garden, the open doors, the air faintly warm. I don't think I was ever tired of being at home. Even after I grew up. I suppose if I had been born a bit earlier I might have stayed at home. Girls did, you know, Kathy. But you could read, instead of fidgeting about. Read what? There are books you haven't read there. Try. Pick one. Plays. I'd read a play. I don't think there are any, her mother said. No. Did father take all the books? Should I read this? Your favourite author. The first novel of a talented new Australian author. Her mother said: It was not his first novel. Kathy held the jacket towards her. That's what it says. No. His first novel wasn't published till later. It was too bitter, I suppose. For the time. They wouldn't publish it. And then they did? Later. Though no one liked it. He wrote it during the war when he wasn't known. I'm going outside, she said. I don't want to read.

I always preferred music, Jessica said.

Your records. And the old seventy-eights. Do you still have them?

I still play them. I've had to keep an old turntable to do it.

Such energy. Up and down all the time. You have everything you want on lp and tapes. Disc. Actually, for your kind of music, you must have a very valuable collection.

It's not a collection, Kathy.

This is a wonderful wine. You're good at these things. I wonder if you should do this play.

Why? You've never read it.

No. Of course not.

Then why do you say that?

I'm not sure. I'm not sure he could write a play. I mean, he's a novelist.

I think this one works. I've only had time to skip, but I think it will. There are different time sequences, some quite a way back, and that will be hard to get. For me. I'm not sure I understand all of it. Yet.

Is it about the war?

Not directly. No, it's no Gallipoli here we go again thing. Our glorious massacres. Oh no. I'm a bit pleased, actually, to have the part. Though I fade out in the last part. But it has some good things.

I suppose he will be there?

There?

Well, rehearsals. That kind of thing.

I doubt it. No one sees him much.

I hope it's a success, Jessica said.

The phone by the bed would ring again. Or go on. The heavy curtains were drawn, the room with little light. There was no clock. It's absurd this thing about time, Helen said. You should see an analyst. It's only in the mornings, Kathy said.

The handpiece was cold. Yes, she said.

It is the middle of the day. Leila's careful voice. Clear. Not to be misunderstood. And you should not be asleep. How is your rehearsal?

It is not mid day. I would be asleep but for people like you. Lousy.

That takes care of everything, then. News for you. He wants to meet you, Kathy. Your favourite playwright.

If I understand what you're saying, I can see him at rehearsal.

Not like that. He suggested lunch or whatever.

But I've never met him.

Your chance, Kathy.

I can't read his books. My mother used to read them. I never really liked them. Not to be a liar, I didn't try that hard.

It doesn't matter. He's quite harmless. In fact he's hardly ever around.
You don't think?
No. Not with him. Nothing like that. Don't be stupid. Formal. He rings me.
Can you come?
That wouldn't be nice, honey.
You're my agent.
Just ring him and that's it.
I don't like writers.
Kathy please.
They shit me. They really do. I'm sick of reading. I don't need them.
You're being very crude. And you don't read.
It's the early morning. I read scripts.
Honey, you're scared. It's not like you.
I'm not.
I think you well may be. So might he. It's his first play. It could go wrong and I suppose that does worry him. Enough to want to talk to you.
Thank you, Leila.

His voice formal. Neutral. Thank you for calling me. I would like to talk.
Yes, she said. I'd be glad to.
Perhaps if we had lunch. Anywhere you like.
Luiges, she said. I often go there. And the view is great. Of the harbour.
Yes. Of the harbour. But you did ask me to suggest a place.
That will be fine.

There was the table and there was the view. She said: Yes. You were right. The harbour.
A little over used, he said. But I'm glad we could meet. I have seen you on television. And two films, I think.

One I liked. The other a quite reasonable disaster. It was more profitable.

Nothing changes. I hope you won't feel like that about this play.

Neutral. She had been right. Tall, very thin, thin grey hair. Neutral in that his battles would be fought inside. She was surprised. Like looking at a script. And then being unsure. She said: That is not a message of confidence.

No.

Are you having doubts about it?

Doubts, yes. He looked at the menu, set it aside. He ordered quickly. He said: This play. I may have tried to write it for the wrong reasons.

Are there any?

There might be.

There's no shortage of wrong plays, she said. They end up as bad television.

About that, I agree. Though I'm a bit surprised to hear someone in the business say so.

A small private treason.

He was looking away beyond her, to the view he seemed to despise, or, she thought, at someone else. What I meant, he said, was that in writing a play I may have tried to project something through real people that I haven't been able to solve in writing fiction. Does that make sense?

I think so. You want to see if they solve it?

It's like trying to see if the people take on another dimension. A dimension beyond myself.

Don't they do that in novels?

To an extent I suppose they do. Possibly this is more or less putting the burden on someone else.

I'm not sure all plays aren't that way. Serious plays.

I'm not suggesting this is some kind of private play. It's meant to be wider than that. I would respect your judgement. The direction the last part takes worries me.

Where it's going. And whether I've been fair to your character. Whether that can be made to work.

There were high bands of clouds, the water shadowed. The boats, she said. People are always sailing boats. I hate them. Yes. I see my own part fairly clearly. I think what you have done towards the end is right. Some things I'm still finding a way into.

I drink too much these days, he said. Who doesn't. But that should not deter us from this wine. Such as?

For me, the man who comes out of the war years. I find it hard to relate to him. My own level of experience, I suppose. My father was in the war. With some distinction, no doubt. I certainly never related to him. Sorry. I just don't know what those years were like.

I'm not sure I do. He looked away, perhaps seeing the other people, the tables. Perhaps timing. Both of them in a scene. Terry's voice. Patient. Resigned. She was suddenly impatient. Memory, he said. Bits and pieces recalled. Probably altered. A great deal lost.

She said: I don't think one has to go too far for that to happen.

No. But a time when you had to make your own certainty. However wrong you were. Very much a matter of perspective. Keeping an identity, I suppose. When everything seemed against that.

I see that. And your character was able to. At a cost?

At a cost.

She leaned forward, the light sudden on her bare arms, her dark hair. Even if, near the end, he is losing control?

I think it does all move away from resolution, rather than towards it. Is that all right?

I think it will be.

I suppose I tend to see things as not resolved.

You mean not just in the play.

Not just in the play.

In the play it forces possibilities in the last part, and that does scare me a bit. I mean, it being open.

It is nothing to scare you. Trust yourself.

And Terry.

I hope. Thinking about identity, what I was trying to say, have you ever seen a painting of James Gleeson's with that name. *Maintenance of Identity*?

No. I don't think so.

You would remember it. In those years I thought I understood that painting. It stayed with me. An image. Just as so many of the paintings of those years moved me profoundly. And still do. I took them into me. I realised later I probably only took a certain amount from Gleeson's painting. Took what I had to, perhaps. I saw it first on the cover of an early *Angry Penguins*. I'm sorry. Don't try to sort that out.

I do see the maintenance of identity. And I'm not sure about it. The woman isn't quite allowed to do that, is she.

I think so. Look, if in a week or so you're still finding that hard, or wrong, please tell Terry. But I would like you to work at what is there, rather than for me to impose a sort of statement on top of the text. Is that all right?

I agree with you about the wine. Splendid. I suppose we do all drink too much. I mean, what else. Yes, fine.

I can talk to both of you about it. Probably I'm hoping you'll find something, show me something that's there.

Perhaps if I had read more of your books it would help. I admit I don't read. I never have. There didn't seem to be time.

Perhaps there was more time once. Maybe we've simply used it up. I suppose I am the books I've read. Sorry if that sounds pompous. But education is so different today. We used to have to discover books. Literally one at a time. No printed lists of recommended reading. And not that many actual books you could put in your hand. I've lived through books, particularly then, when I was young. Lived very acutely and strongly. They were experience.

I'm sorry. I didn't mean to deluge you with these sad stories. But it has something to do with this play.

She looked out across the still water, the high land beyond crowded with buildings. He said: I've got worried about novels. Reading used to be a private experiencing. It made, I suppose, certain demands. Often heavy demands. Now people are simply less open to that, everything is groups, public reading. An easy response. And not a lonely one. That is, where you can talk about response at all.

Yes, she said. And of course that has made a difference to theatre.

I simply wonder if I should forget about words. This play may be a sort of half way house. As I say, written for the wrong reasons.

Not wrong, she said. No. And about books, I agree. I know I should have read more. My mother has always read your books, there were some in the house, so no excuse. Though I'd have to admit she was no great reader. Especially later. She was too busy, too.

Everyone is. I'm glad she read the books. And I look forward to seeing how you handle my rather lost character.

Lost maybe. But strong. As I see it.

I can't stay, Helen said. Tell Leila I'm sorry I missed her.
I think that's her now, she said.
We'll meet on the doorstep. See you.
Sorry, Leila said. One of those days. Can I have a drink?
You always do.
How was it?
As a lunch, fine. If that's what you mean. I think you were right. He's not very sure about the play.
It's the ones that are dead sure you have to worry about, Kathy.
True. But I think you were right. In your tactful way. I was a bit scared. I do scare. I don't know why.

We all do, honey.

Not you, Leila. But it was easy to talk to him. He listens. It was all very surface. I suppose it would be, but I just had the feeling most of him is locked away.

Never knock that. I get a life story a day.

Perhaps he wants this play to make him some money. Would his books make much?

Not all that much. You're right, he's never given out a lot. I think he's supposed to have had an interest in a farm in Western Australia. Some weird place. At one time. You'd know it. Your homeland. And he worked for a paper here. Still does features. He gets by. He does things on environment. The great outback. Falling to pieces. For mine it can't fall apart too quick. You'd have seen them.

I don't read newspaper stuff.

Lucky.

Leila, where can I see a Gleeson painting?

Are you going to collect paintings?

In here? He talked about it at lunch.

Ask him.

I didn't like to.

I don't know honey. I just don't know. But there are plenty of galleries.

And books. It all seemed important to him. Well, bugger books.

Kathy, this is not a play about him.

He did write it.

I'm not sure what the problem is.

Okay, so perhaps we helped each other out a bit about the play. Talking. But I had this idea somehow he wanted to see me. Vet me? I don't know.

You have the part. You're my client. He couldn't do anything. Let him try.

No. I don't mean that. No. In a way I liked him. Even though I don't think you'd ever know him. There's a lot sort of shut away. He reminded me of mother. Sort of just didn't care. Goes off. Sorry. You wouldn't understand, never having met my mother.

Most of my brood of clients are very oncoming. Very open. Very demonstrative. You'd be surprised what I hear. In the day's work. He'd be a break. I think you're just right for this play. Don't worry.

The sprinkler made a curtain above the green lawn. An extension of the glass, almost. The idea with its own comfort. She touched the pane. From the window the street was deserted. Further down, where the road turned, almost certainly Mr Mark weeding his lawn. Despite the heat. Here the hard light not much softened by the even spray of water, the greenness to the roadside. Richard had insisted. It's too much for you, Jessica. Worrying about the garden. This system will be completely automatic. You need not worry at all. I will not even have to go out there, she said. All the street green to the road's edge. Lawn. A few street trees. It's like a backdrop, Kathy said. You in that sun dress. Not hiding anything against the window. Nice, really. In one of his books, the third one, I think, Jessica said, there was a description of a woman standing by a window. She had taken her clothes off. They were about to make love. I remember I saw you reading that page. When you were still at school. The things parents remember, Kathy said. It's frightening. Did I finish the book? You were not very good at finishing books. No, I wasn't. But perhaps I was reminded of that when I saw you standing there. I must have been, because you picked it up, too. Bloody books. I don't like people inside my head. Both of them laughing. The words in the empty room. Little more than the silence of mid day. The heat. The sprinkler and the clean lawn. The hills along the side of the bay. Bare trees against the sky, the light sharp behind them, but fading. The hills fading so the folds hardly showed. What are you looking at, he said. She did not move. I don't know. The evening, I suppose. The hills, he said. If I was a painter. It is easier for them. He touched her and then stood away and he said: In that light you are becoming like the shadow. Are you there? You haven't gone somewhere through the glass? His hands on her hips, along her back, turning her. There were people in the street. A car.

In that other room, the upstairs window open, the old house with its sounds of people, and she knew they were nearly ready for the evening meal, to dine, as her mother always said. Across the paddocks, away across to Joyce's place, the land clear in the late summer, shadowed, but not dark. To dine early, for Charles to get back on time. We will have to go to the house, she said. His hands touching her back. I have to show it to you. I don't think we will ever do that, he said. The sprinkler system on the lawn, regular, even, Richard proud of it. Part of the way he organised things. By the small clock on the mantel almost time she went back to town. To the shops. You don't have to work there now, Richard said. You have very good people working for you. You can stay here. Travel, if that is what you would like. Thank you Richard, she said. But I am not Kathy. The words almost said.

The lights at the corner held, the traffic unbroken. A light rain drifted. Like the exhaust haze. He saw the woman, looking at him. He said: It has to be. Leslie.

I knew it was you.

They crossed with the changing lights, moved in towards the shop front. He said: I wasn't thinking. Or I'd have seen you earlier.

The traffic, she said. I'm not that keen on the city these days.

Not much like we knew. Or not in some ways. I'm not sure it's changed otherwise. Give or take that on the streets I can't always be sure what country I'm in. And some fine old buildings.

Like we lived in.

I'd like to think they preserved that place. You don't know?

I never went back.

I was going to lunch, he said. You can't simply walk away down Bourke Street. Would you have time for lunch?

Oh yes. A few things I have to get. After will do.

There's a reasonable place. Collins Street. Probably quicker if we walk.

He asked for a table out of the way, near the wall, the windows at one end partly curtained, a narrow view of the street. It was quiet. She looked about with a kind of amusement, a cynicism he remembered.

Not much like where I used to work.

Is that place still there?

I've never looked.

I come here sometimes, he said. Publishers. The occasional editor. When I have business here.

You don't live here. We'd have met before this.

Sydney. For better or worse. A born again city. By new witchdoctors. A grisly process.

I remember, she said. You said you would be going. You don't like it?

I don't think I care. I suppose I could live anywhere now. I did like it very much at first. Exciting, I seemed to belong. Sounds a bit trite now, but I had a room up at the Cross for a while. People were interesting, it was alive. Well, it's all in the literature now, I suppose. A revered cliche. There was a small place just off Darlinghurst Road I used to have my evening meal. About the only one of the day, actually. You could sit by the window and just watch. People. I haven't been there for years.

I know what you mean. I did wander about there on a holiday one time.

I'm a fair way out now. In fact I don't think I live anywhere. I don't belong at all. In today's Sydney I'm not even an outsider. And that's a crime.

You were always a bit that, she said.

It's odd, but the place where you used to work was a lot more honest than this place, or what's around today.

If you didn't look out the back. But yes.

I don't look out the back of these places.

There wasn't all that much of it around.

Sorry?

Honesty. Even then.

No. But there was some. Whatever side you were on.

She looked at the menu, ordered quickly, then said: Or whatever you like.

Whatever you like, he said. I generally drink too much at these places.

Not hard. She said suddenly: It was always sides for you, wasn't it. Then.

She had not changed so much. Filled out. Something in her face that had made Robert sketch her, and later paint her, did she know that, still there, the tiredness that had kept her asleep in the mornings in the lines from her eyes. About her lips.

Yes, he said. I suppose it was.

Now?

Now I don't know what the sides are. And you, you haven't really changed. You live in Melbourne?

I got married. Two kids. I don't know how it happened.

Did you know Michael Robert painted a portrait of you? You remember that night? Exhibited it. *Head of a girl.*

No? Some girl.

If you put a different emphasis on that, I'd agree.

Not like you. But thanks.

It was good. Someone bought it. It's in a book on his work.

Someone bought the painting?

Michael made the big time. I knew he would. At some cost, he gave up his job after the war, but he did.

You used to know quite a few painters.

There were quite a few around. And a lot fewer phoneys than now.

You knew more of them than writers. Didn't you.

Yes. Some writers. But what the painters were doing fitted somehow with the way I saw things then. You know, I didn't respond critically to any of that painting. Though even then there was something beginning to be written about it. I simply responded to the paintings somehow. Their part in a time. What was happening. An emotional experience. For me, a kind of wonder. After all that has been written since, all the analysis, the explanation, I don't suppose it's possible to see them like that again. I was naive. But I'm glad.

You were certainly wrapped up in it all.

Perhaps more than anything since. But I did know more painters. They were more open, I think. I find writers different. I still don't know many.

What are you doing?

Writing. A few things.

Same as you were.

If anything is the same as it was.

That's for sure. I'm afraid I don't read anything. Not even the bloody papers.

Can't

Don't.

He laughed, moved his hand suddenly as if he would

touch hers. Leslie, I'm very glad we met. Let's eat all this food and drink as much as we like.

What could be better. She said suddenly: That other painter, the one who did the painting you had, is he still around?

Very much. Jackson is quite famous. His work's changed a bit. Or widened out. He hasn't changed. I was with him yesterday. So I should have known I'd see you today. These things go in pairs.

But you haven't seen me before. When you've seen him.

More often he comes to Sydney. You're not any easier to convince about anything, Leslie. Jackson never forgot you always turned his painting to the wall.

Don't tell him you met me.

We're doing a trip inland in a week or so. I'm doing a piece on erosion. Environment. That kind of thing. More people read these things today than ever read novels. I'm not sure that it's going to make any difference. Not now. But it depresses the hell out of me.

That people read that and not novels?

No. No, I don't care about them reading or not reading novels. Not any more. No. The kind of bloody total disaster this country is set for. The cynical destruction. The pious lipservice. But forget it. Blame Jackson.

You think I should?

He wouldn't mind. But oddly enough it's even forced him outward, away from his buildings and streets. Though they did pull down his one time studio. All that area. But he's done some very strong images of a wrecked landscape. He tries to shrug them off. But they're there.

It was enough to keep going, she said. Then. Without all that. You know, I never found anyone to make tea for me in the morning. When you went.

I'm glad. Not your husband?

He was a carpenter. Did quite well. A builder now. No. The bugger used to get away in the dark most mornings.

Not so bad now, but no, that's not exactly his kind of thing.

I'm sorry about that. If you want a replacement.

I'll remember. You talking of Robert, what happened to his bitchy girl friend?

Her. She keeps with a pretty fair determination to the fringes of literary groups.

I see.

Yes.

With him?

Yes. Something they're both bitter about. But yes.

She said: I think you have changed. A bit. Not much.

I should have. I look out into those streets and there's a freedom there none of us ever knew. Not when we were the age of those people. And the ironic thing is I don't think our bloody war had anything to do with it.

Maybe you haven't changed. Then, sort of no one was going to get in your way.

I don't know. I think then, everything got in my way.

He watched her lift her glass. Her arm bare in the loose coat, fuller, but still her fine clear skin. He said: But perhaps all the doubts have had time to gather.

I think I see what you mean. Now.

But it had to be like that. Then. I'm sure of that at least.

She said: After the last time I saw you, the old bastard died, and they had the place up for auction. I had to move. Rather funny, if I'd been a tenant in the house I'd have had rights. But they wanted to forget about that place down the back. I never thought I'd miss it, but I did. I missed you going, too, and I didn't expect that.

Leslie we should just walk out of here and go away for a week somewhere.

Leave the old man.

And the kids.

They have left.

No problem.

Who would you leave?

I don't think I have anyone to leave.

I'm not sure what I should say about that.

Don't say anything. Shall we risk some more wine?

I think I must go, she said. She reached across the table, her hand resting quickly on his. I'm not sure I believe this. But great. Thanks.

Long shadows from the house angled across the clear ground towards the trees along the fence. Across the rise beyond, the frames of houses held the light, the skeletons of roofs, of walls, the ground broken, heaps of builder's rubble, sand, bricks.

They're getting close, Jackson said. If that piece of land by the fence is sold they'll be on me. Fucking developers. Why don't you want to go?

I told you. I get up there and I see what has been done to that country, what's still being done, and I get pissed in shithouse pubs. If you see what I mean.

We get pissed every time you come down here. I read the articles you did on the gold mining boom in your home State a while back. Balanced. Reasonable. Quite good.

Balanced reasonable when the editors had finished with them. They wouldn't use part of what I said about the open cut mining for gold. I rather like the old gold towns, wrecked shafts, a few often very interesting old buildings, fascinating junk about the ground. The odd poppet head. The land coming back over it all. Nothing will ever come back over these open cuts. They will be much worse than woodchipping.

Everything will be left clean and tidy.

I did think once we might work something out. Living in this country. I allowed for stupidity. Greed. We were a bit apologetic about greed. But I didn't realise there would be a pride in being greedy.

You're scared of this inland trip.

You could put it that way.

But you are going.

I have to go. I have to write something, even if only part of it gets through.

I have felt like that about painting. Not so much of late years, admitted. It's been easier.

Where I'm supposed to go is the most barbaric area of Australia. Far western New South. Into Queensland. I'll be pissed every night. And they'll edit it out to balanced development. Harsh country. Pioneering spirit.

They'll let you get away with a bit more than that. You're a crafty bastard.

It's getting hard. The last time I visited the ancestral home, and it was the last, I found them in the middle of crop spraying. I admit the reality was a bit of a shock. I mean, so close to home. I did some research, came up with names, quantities, areas, effects, pesticide in use in other countries. A fine strong piece. No one would touch it.

You can't expect to undermine the morning breakfast rituals. I'll come with you on this run and do some painting. I think I can get something from that kind of country. I need a change.

It's all going sour, he said. I don't like much of the painting that's about today. Play school stuff to keep the men off the streets. I'm getting old. But you said once that if writing was bad enough, someone would read it. It seems to me now that if painting is bad enough someone will write about it.

Inside this stockade I might agree with you.

He got up and stepped towards the edge of the verandah. He turned back to the chair. I don't think I will walk anywhere. Just sit here and watch the sun go down.

I do some of that, Jackson said.

It's a good place you've got here. Worth the move from your inner city cave.

It's not going to be good when they ride over the hill at

me. They're coming. But your article. Maybe what you write about things is a bit savage.

It has to be.

And about people?

What you paint about people can be more savage than anything I write.

They'll take it in paint. It's the old thing. Hang it on the wall. Look at the dollar sign. As long as the price is high enough. I get a laugh out of it. No bastard would buy my stuff once. As you know.

There's been some hearty rubbish put about on those years, one way and another. But I haven't seen much about the way it was.

The way some of it was. Nothing.

The way some of it was. No.

With the painting, they didn't want to know about anything to do with that time. In fact they never really wanted to admit a lot of that kind of painting, what it was about wasn't admitted until that Art And Social Commitment show. It was safe then.

I walked round that for hours. Several days.

Then, I didn't care whether people bought or not. That was their affair. But I cared about some of the things that were said about my work. Now if the bastards want to buy, they pay. It's getting bloody dark out here.

Who wants to see.

I had convictions once. For a while.

You still do. And a cynic might say when your painting began to sell you got a different slant.

Been said.

Of course.

Every bloody thing's been said. As you ought to know. You can't go on writing. It's finished. I can still paint.

You should spread that more widely. About writing.

I do. No bugger listens.

We are getting pissed.

Wasn't that what you came for?

I came to talk to you.

Same thing. We'll go on this bloody journey. See what comes of it. We could do a book. No editing.

No publisher.

I'll get some bastard.

The bar was quiet. A long spread of light from the small coloured frames of the window brought a faint glow from the old carpet. She stood in the doorway of the small cubicle that no one ever seemed to occupy. She had a loose long sleeved dress, patterned in colours that were like the light against the windows, her hair drawn back. She wore no makeup. She said: Why this place?

I'll get you a drink.

Waiting for a tram. Right down here. What goes on?

He put the glass on the table. For a moment he thought she was going to refuse it. Then she drank quickly. Careless of who might see. In this empty room. She said: You silly bugger.

I wasn't sure about the house. I wanted to see what had happened.

You can come to the house. Better than here.

I wasn't sure.

Nothing has happened.

Nothing?

Do you want another drink?

I'll get it, he said.

She leaned across the table. The house would be better

than this. But there's no one here, I suppose. Harry didn't die.

I saw that car.

You can forget that. He's just gone away.

It wasn't my fault, he said. If you're trying to get at me.

I know it wasn't your fault. Or anything to do with you. Two characters called. Very smooth. Harry had to go interstate. They weren't sure when he'd be back. It might be some time. I wasn't to worry. I'd be looked after. So I took the money. Contribution for the poor. And they pissed off.

They don't know about me.

I'd say not.

I looked in the papers and there wasn't anything.

Nothing happened.

The police line is that what they are working isn't happening. I don't know who they pay high enough up for that to be. But no one wants to know.

So, nothing to get away with.

They'll find who did it, he said. And no one will know about that either.

I don't know where it leaves me.

Being careful.

I'm always careful.

I'm sorry, Rene.

We can't do anything. And it looks like you're clear.

I couldn't be sure.

If you want to come to the house it's quite okay. She put the glass down. It's what they'd expect.

The words made their own patterns, lifting from the clean lines, hazed, falling away, angled. Finding their own way. Old counters in their own ceremony. She was coming towards the desk and briefly the words took shape. Her white dress, the slash of black across the shoulders, her small hat, dark, at an angle. From the darkness of the walls, the tables and shaded lights. A focus hardening. She leaned towards him. Her face pale, made up in a kind of perfection. A film scene. Her hair touching her shoulders. She said: I'm sorry. I've disturbed you.

Jessica, he said. No. You didn't disturb me. The pages had all gone surrealistic. I thought I was watching a film.

She stood by the desk, looking down at him, her hands about a small white handbag. He said: Are all your handbags white?

White. No. I have a black one.

For night.

Is it?

Have you come to read?

To find you.

Perhaps we should go. I've finished here.

Outside, in the sudden light, he said: I think you've startled that room for the day. Reminded them. Of how dangerous those shelves are.

It was a terrible thing to do. If you want to go back?

I'd have been going anyway.

We could have tea somewhere? Would you like to come to my place? We can get a tram. Before the rush. I got away early.

He helped her up the low steps of the tram, herself light, moving easily. He said: How did you know I was at the library?

I didn't. But you said you read there some afternoons. I hadn't seen you. I did look in at that exhibition of war artists.

Official war artists.

I think so.

Rather staid.

Oh. Was it? I liked some of the painting.

By comparison. Oddly it all seemed calmer, more removed somehow than painting of life in the streets. Than those other paintings we saw. As if the madness wasn't in the war at all.

The stairs led up from a small hallway. A narrow landing, the room wide, light, long windows on one side, thinly curtained, a finely patterned wallpaper. He could not remember a house with wallpaper. Even his aunt's house. It seemed the fashion of another age, from illustrations in books. There were two easy chairs, a small lounge with heavy cushions, a low table. Two doors from the room, one open to the kitchen. She was watching him.

Do you like it?

Yes, he said. I'm afraid a bit beyond my experience of flats.

She opened the door of the other room, he saw for a moment a dressing table, a wide mirror, the room light. She was taking off the dark hat, touching her hair before the mirror.

On the walls a few paintings, landscapes, a print of a Robert Johnson, a foreground of trees, a river, going back to a blue distance. Another of trees and a long stretch of light on very clear water, old, heavy framed. A watercolour of a fine two storey house, part of old brick outbuildings, trees along a slope of rising land. Magazines on the low table. A cabinet gramophone, shelves that might hold records. He looked briefly at the magazines, a *Walkabout, Vogue, Mademoiselle*, what looked like a trade magazine of materials and design.

She brought the tea things on an old silver-railed tray, the china with a simple, red pattern reminding him of his aunt's cups, plates, jugs, a large teapot, that stood on the dresser in the dark kitchen. Dusted, perhaps removed and handled. She said: What is it?

Your tray, the tea things, I was suddenly thinking of my aunt. Where I used to live. She had shelves of china. But I don't think we used them.

These are from home.

The house in that watercolour.

How did you know?

It had to be. Do you go there often?

When I can. I'm sorry if I interrupted your work this afternoon.

No. You caused something of a sensation in there. You were very beautiful. I didn't believe you myself at first.

Oh. Have you been busy?

Yes. In an ill directed way.

Why is it ill directed?

Because it has to be.

Because of the war.

That complicates it. Yes.

Trying to write.

That's part of it. And trying to know. You could say trying to find what there is to know. I don't even know what I have to know.

You make it very complicated.

It should be simple. Except it's not. I was lucky, I went to a university. I think then I was simply trying to find some kind of understanding. And I did begin to find it.

And the war stopped that.

It did indeed. I'm sorry if this sounds very pompous.

No. I think I know what you mean. It isn't how I'd see my own life. But I respect someone who has to do things. Who knows what they have to do. This sounds silly perhaps, but I admire Joyce for that. She's quite mad sometimes, but she is sure what she is going to do.

Horses.

You're laughing at me. I know that seems a rather crazy jump from what you were saying.

No. Probably the same in the end.

You think?

I'm sorry I couldn't come and meet her that time.

I'm glad you came now, she said. I was afraid you wouldn't. I missed not seeing you lately.

Things have been a bit mixed up.

We could have dinner. I could cook something. Would that be all right?

That would be very all right. But not if it's any trouble.

I cook for myself. Much nicer if I share it.

He went with her to the shops in the main street, she said there was time before they closed. She had been going anyway. He was unsure whether to pay for the food, unwilling to embarrass her in shops where she was obviously known. Aware this was not the kind of place he shopped, but she seemed unselfconscious, talking to him, at times concentrating on the things before her on the counter, goods on shelves. In the flat they put the things in the kitchen and she said: There's almost nothing to drink. Some wine, but we should keep that for the meal? Friends were here in the weekend. It's all got so hard to find.

Do you have people often?

Not really. Friends. People connected with the shop.

Dresses.

Rag trade. I work with Mrs Lyon. I told you. Designing is what I want to do. She has a defence contract for some stuff, so she can keep the machines going and gets a lot of other things made up. She's doing very well.

This seems to be a city of defence contracts. And you?

After the war I want to have my own place.

She worked quickly, but in a more complicated way than he had been used to. He could think of no other word. Ingredients, the way she performed what he had thought of as simple tasks, cutting, preparing, dishes, utensils. Without haste. Very sure. He laughed. She said: What is it?

If your dress designing doesn't go well enough you could be a cook.

I like cooking. I always cook at home. I always have done since I was a child. She said: After the war. Do you think it will be a good time for what you want to do?

For you, yes. For me, I wish I knew. Oddly enough now

is a good time, in one way. Writing. Painting. Some new publishing. A real vigour. Exciting. As if it's all going somewhere. But there's enormous opposition. Academic vested interest. And plain fear. Some academics sit in their classical dunnies and simply void over everything in any way new.

Good heavens.

They might be very powerful after the war. I don't know. They won't give up easily.

It will be material things, she said. My father says that. People I talk to now.

He's probably right. And they.

If it's dresses, clothes, I hope he is. He doesn't like the war.

Who does.

Some people. Mrs Lyon. Charles.

Charles?

A man I know. In the Air Force.

He likes that?

Well, somehow the whole thing, I think. Being an officer. Having rank. Part of something that's sort of all organised. Is it unfair to say that?

Not unfair at all. I might envy him.

I'll set the table in here, she said. It's good having a kitchen like this. Do you envy him?

It's a double edged thing, he said. I don't know.

On the landing, the only other door opened to the bathroom, clean, ordered, the built-in bath and gas heater. Shower. The old claw legged bath of his aunt's bathroom, the wooden floor not quite covered with lino, the old heater, as if someone had put it there and forgotten to come back. For so many years. This an illustration from glossy magazines. The table in the other room.

She had changed to a plain white dress, sleeveless, her hair brushed smooth, parted cleanly. As she sat across the table from him it was, again, something from a film. A magazine advertisement. She said: What are you thinking about?

Films. This.

You look very serious.

I keep seeing magazines.

In here?

Us in magazines.

And in films?

Yes.

Do you mind?

No I don't. And you are a very good cook.

I'm glad about that, anyhow.

She brought coffee into the other room. Real, she said. Mrs Lyon. She seems able to get all sorts of things.

There's a reasonable business in getting them.

I suppose there is. Do you like music?

I'm a musical illiterate, he said. Unfortunately.

I probably am myself. I only like some things. I mean, I get restless with long orchestral pieces, that kind of thing. I like quartets. Piano. Harpsichord, yes, very much. Eighteenth century, I suppose. Baroque.

There was a lecturer at the university who said if you listened to the music of the eighteenth century you knew what a great century that was.

I'm sure about the music. Was it a great century?

If you had his perspective, yes.

I found this recording of Telemann, she said. It's not very good. Shall I play it?

She stood by the gramophone. He said: Yes. Though I know nothing of him.

The intricate pattern of sound moved in the quiet room, and he was reminded of words, somewhere, eluding him. She watched him, as if he might not like the music. When the brief recording was finished she said: I have this of Bach. A better recording, but they go together.

She had no regard of him now. Withdrawn. Then in the

silence she said: It's so beautiful. Always. But words don't make sense.

There's a passage of Aldous Huxley about Bach I was trying to think of. A response in words. A translation, I suppose. It fascinated me.

I don't read very much, she said. I never have. I've always liked music. We have a piano at the old house. I've played since I was a child. Not well, unfortunately.

You would miss that, here.

I have a friend who says that after the war there will be big changes in recording. All sorts of new materials. And sound reproduction. He's in radio communication, so perhaps he's right.

He probably would be. Our brave new world. Before I came over here I saw a task force using American machinery to clear an airstrip. In what I'd thought of as fairly well timbered country. Bulldozers. I'm not sure I understand yet what that is going to mean.

It will make things easier, surely.

It will indeed. It's just I hadn't seen anything on that scale before. You grow up, I suppose. But your friend. You have a lot of friends.

In a way.

In a way?

I sometimes think I don't know people. Joyce says I escape. Into music. Designing. The work I do. It shouldn't be like that.

It makes sense, he said. Probably much better.

Do you think you could find me the piece about Bach?

It describes how a man, coming into a room, actually hears Bach being played, hears in a physical sense, physiological if you like, a bit of literary showmanship, but very good. And there's a piece that's hard to put accurately, Huxley is suggesting Bach as a poet meditating on truth and beauty. As a subject that might alarm some poets, no doubt. But he says the music encompasses everything, admits everything, all the contradictions of the world, evil, brutality, sadness, and consolation. Yet it affirms that everything somehow is right. Acceptable. Can be accepted.

Do you agree with that?

As an idea, not in any part.

For Bach's music?

For the music you might be able to say that. If you say you can put music into words. I don't know the music well enough. Don't know it at all.

I think you could say that. Yes. I think he is right.

I haven't put it as persuasively as Huxley. Who could? It's in *Point Counter Point*. But I'd prefer what Maugham says of Bach in a story. He speaks of a warm scent of the soil, and a sturdy strength that seems to have its roots deep in the earth. And he says something of an elemental power that is timeless.

Yes.

Though it's a bit ironic to be thinking of anything timeless at the moment.

We have to think of it. We must.

Cling to it, then.

Do you think we could go to a concert? I mean, would you like to come?

Now?

No of course not. One evening.

Yes. But there are problems.

Why?

I haven't got clothes for social occasions. That kind of thing.

It's not a social occasion.

Not for you.

She seemed suddenly close to tears, surprising him so that he did not know what to say, she had turned her head, it might have been a movement of the light. She said: I'm sorry. I'm very clumsy. But it wouldn't be an occasion.

Not like that. Not at all. Just music.
   Then yes, he said.

She was tidying the tables, the cafe empty. Stranger, she said.
   Am I too late? I'm hungry. Anything solid. Please.
   No one's too late here. For the leftovers. You don't look so good.
   Problems.
   Well, she said, they say it might all be over before long.
   She went into the back. The cafe clean enough. But worn. Everything used too long. Chipped and marked with use. In the evenings they had all been in the kitchen, his mother and sister setting out the meal, the day lost in the early darkness, but shaped behind them. Perhaps it would never be gone. Shaped beyond loss. She stood by the table and he said: Is it still your afternoon off?
   That's what they call it.
   Why don't we go and have a drink.
   Why don't we.
   There were never many people in the weekday afternoons, the small room off the passage deserted, smelling of the past night's smoke and beer. She said: What will you do when it ends?
   If it ends. Find some kind of work.
   Are you making out?
   More or less. Some ways, less. Papers might be a problem later. Like bloody coupons now.
   You're short?
   I'm not sure who to ask now. I tried one character I was pretty sure of where I work Saturdays, but he backed off. I'm a bit worried there's something out there.
   To do with Harry?
   Could be. Could be anything.
   Some ways it has got hard. The MPs shot a man down the road from here. A negro. Deserter, been living just a

block away.

With a woman?

I knew her. She comes in here.

The Americans don't muck about.

He was running. He didn't have a gun. She says they shoot them when they can.

I don't know how it will end. Or how to get that far.

Coupons, I can get you some.

Just a few, he said. If you have them. It's stupid. I know they're out there. But since Harry I have to be careful.

Keep it that way.

Right.

But it's a while now. Nothing.

No. It didn't happen.

I'm glad you came, she said. I feel like drinking. I'm sick of this place. And the old bastard is all jitters. Something's wrong. I mightn't be there much longer.

You can come in with me.

Thanks. But I couldn't go all that way out there.

It's not all that way out there.

Too far.

You might get a job out there. No travelling.

I've just about made it, she said. Till the whole fucking thing ends. I don't want strife. Thanks, though.

At six o'clock they went out onto the street, the long shadows, the sudden cold. She said: Let's go home.

She opened the door from the lane. The narrow room unchanged. Make us one of your cups of tea. It's all there is. But there's this after. She put the bottle of whisky on the table.

American.

Who else would have it.

Do we need the tea?

Yes we do.

I don't think I'm going to be well, he said.

When she lay on the bed she had taken off only her skirt.

She twisted at her blouse. I'm tired. I can't be bothered with this thing. I don't think I can get it off. Rub my shoulders. Please.

You're scared of the cold.

Why not.

His fingers moved slowly across her shoulders, her back, her skin colouring faintly. An ebb of colour. She moved her hand to the light switch. He lay across her in the narrow bed.

Wake up you useless bugger, she said. You can't sleep there.

I have to.

Just keep me warm. I'll settle for that. It's all I'll get. She moved to the edge of the bed and he slid across to the wall. Drinking makes me cold. Maybe you should move back in here.

In the late afternoon he heard the woman shouting at the child. The pile of paper on the table, the loose sheets on a strip of cardboard writing pad. Dulling, in the light from the side window, as if the shadows across the broken patches of lawn moved into the room. Paper. Dead. For now. Perhaps for ever. Dropped from that window it would sink into the small space between fence and wall. Hardly blow away. Layer of a midden. Of other tenants. Twisted empty tooth paste tubes, a jar of cold cream, scraps of wrapping, cough mixture bottle, a condom half held by a broken cardboard box. A midden to grow for ever. Enfolding the house. And those inside it. He took his coat, locked the inner door, though it was likely there was another key to that, closed the heavy door to the verandah. The street was deserted. The voices of children from one of the houses rising in sudden violence, then laughing. The evening crowds filled the station, flushes of people along the platforms, the overhead walks, thinning across the pavements. He did not phone. He stood by the door, waited, if there were people he could go. She might not be there. She was standing in the doorway, the door held, the small entrance hall with its old hat stand, the cap and walking stick. He said: I thought it might be the old people.

They wouldn't hear, she said.

Is it all right?

Of course. I didn't know you were coming.

Her hips slender, rounded, moving only slightly in the thin white dress as she went up the stairs ahead of him, her body held straight, her hand touching the rail. Moving lightly, easily. He said: Has anyone ever fallen down these stairs?

Fallen down them? I don't know.

In the room he looked at the thinly curtained window, the shape of roofs, trees, darkening. She drew the heavier curtains.

A drink? Not much choice, I'm afraid.

No. No thanks.

I don't seem very good as a drink provider lately.

It's been scarce, he said.

It's very humiliating. I have to rely on Mrs Lyon. Though she's good about it.

Is she.

I was going to a concert.

By yourself.

Yes.

You're a strange person.

I've never minded going out alone. Being alone, if that's what you mean.

But then no doubt you'd have met some of your friends there.

I might have.

It's a city of music, he said. Across the desert where I come from, if there was a concert it would be too bad to go to.

I'll get us something to eat. Would you like to hear a record? Anything you like.

No. It's all right.

She said: You don't really know what to do. Do you?

That sums it up. Probably better than you realise.

I might realise.

I'm in a certain amount of trouble. A few things. But it's not your concern.

Her face held sudden strain, a fear. As if she was a child an adult was about to taunt. I'm not much good to you, am I.

You don't have to go about being good for people.

No. I'll get something to eat. Are you in a hurry?

I don't think so.

He picked up the fashion magazine from the table. Good paper. Colour. Well set. Austerity at least passing this by. He stood in the doorway of the kitchen.

I'm not in a hurry. If you don't throw me out. I'm sorry.

She did not say anything and he said: Perhaps later it will work out. I seem to live for a later. But I'm not sure it will be any better. It has to be.

We have been promised a better world.

Indeed we have.

You're laughing at me. But at least it will be good for us. People like Mrs Lyon and myself. I'm sure of it. People are only waiting.

Waiting to go on where they left off. I'm afraid you may be right.

I'll be able to cook you very splendid meals. And we'll have anything we want to drink.

I can't wait. But your meals are splendid.

Can I ask you a question? It's not being vain. Do you think I'm the best cook you've known?

That's a very devious question. But yes. By far.

She laughed, for a moment the happiness of her expression surprised him. Easily, he said.

You worry about your writing, she said. Perhaps too much?

Perhaps. Maybe I need some greater commitment.

I should think you were completely committed. In what you want to do.

Social commitment. An involvement. Perhaps I should join the Party.

The communists?

Yes.

Surely you don't want to be like them.

What are they like?

I don't know.

But I don't want involvement. Groups of people. No. And a lot of the writers and painters have left the Party. There's a vast amount of argument, and I don't think that is any kind of good for me. But I'm not sure what is.

She said: I've managed to get a very beautiful Beethoven recording. A quartet. Would you like to hear it? Later?

The music hard to follow, drawing him almost at once in to it, as if it fitted his mood, haunting, full of dark undertones, a surge that impelled, and invoked resistance, disturbing him so that he was not sorry when the music ended, when her quiet, unobtrusive movement to change the sides was over and she stood looking down at him.

Disturbing, he said. Dark.

If you want to feel that, yes.

I think it frightens me. I wonder what Huxley would have to say about that.

Some of the paintings you've shown me have made me feel like that.

I suppose so.

I'm trying to get a new recording I've heard about. The *Triple Concerto*. Would you listen to it?

Is it like that?

No. It's quite wonderful. I don't mean the quartet isn't. You're confusing me.

When will you have it?

Perhaps by the weekend. But I forgot. It can't be the weekend.

Later.

Next week is, oh I don't know.

I don't have any claim on your time. We can listen to the recording whenever you say.

But you do, she said. You do. I want you to. But Charles is coming on ten day's leave.

Your squadron leader.

I have to see him.

Of course.

You're offended.

Of course I'm not.

I can see you are.

You tell me I am something. I tell you I'm not.

It won't matter if you go.

I know that.

Oh god. Of course it will. Please. I knew it was wrong when you came tonight.

It hasn't been wrong. I needed to talk to someone.

And I was there.

You were there. What else can someone be. It's all a bloody mess. Some things are going beyond me. Forget that. Charles. Do you have some kind of arrangement with him. Can I ask that?

Yes.

Are you going to marry him? Or just a casual thing.

Not casual. No.

I didn't think it would be. Not with you.

He thinks we are going to be married.

And you?

I don't know.

There's no difficulty about next week. I'm hardly in a position to be in the way of your squadron leader.

You resent this, don't you.

I might resent him. If I did it wouldn't matter. And don't cry. You can't cry about a thing like this. Surely.

I don't know what sort of a thing like this it is. I can't help crying.

He touched her arm, gently, she let herself come against him, still, a tension held, lessened, but that he did not attempt to influence. He said: Is he your lover?

Perhaps in the way you mean.

Is there another way?

Yes there is.

I see.

I haven't found it, she said. However stupid that sounds.

I shouldn't have said that.

But you did.

You unsettled me.

Surprised you, you mean.

Do I?

Because you and I haven't been lovers.

We haven't been to bed together, he said. I've not questioned that.

I know. I'm just clumsy. I told you.

You're not clumsy. Or if you are it doesn't matter. You're very beautiful.

You're laughing at me. But it's better than being angry with me.

All this is the fault of your quartet, he said.

She laughed suddenly. How strange. But you will come and listen to the concerto. We could have a dinner party. Perhaps four of us. Could you bring someone?

I don't think I could. And I'm not sure that's a very good idea.

I expect not. But you will come? Later?

Later.

The music was lost, sound, movement. The noise of the

train its own sound. The movement of people. Their sudden disagreement without bitterness. Without anger. Without the sudden violence of feeling. Remembered. Barbara, they had not fought often, but in sharp anger. Like hate. And with clear regrets. The evening he had left her room, gone down the street to the corner, there was no tram and he began walking. Then stopped. Turning back. Near the corner she was walking towards him. A jacket over her thin dress. And they clung to one another on the footpath, clear in the light of the intersection, the laughter from a passing car. Here the carriage, the closed windows, a man asleep in the corner. The elderly woman. Here the girl with her house. In a countryside he had never seen, and which she did not live in. Three men moved against the darkness of the heavy scrub and the few high salmon gums. The girl coming from the house by the siding each night to their camp. The rabbiters working eroded paddocks pocked and cratered. One night the girl not returning to the small house. The rabbiters moved about their work. The lines of skins. Gutted bodies in the truck. The father walking the thick scrub behind the old dam. Away from the men, from their camp. For days in which they said nothing. The ants about her clothing. The flies. There were the police. And there was no secret. But the rabbiters had never seen her and the girl's parents refusing to say she had ever gone out at night. Ever left the house that fronted the bare station yard. The police knowing. But the rabbiters did not know the girl. Save to have seen her. The three of them. All or none. The rabbiters moved on. The darkness, the shadows of the buildings, the faint light of the iron roof of the station. Long a part of childhood. And here the house, framed, unchanging, from the wall of her pleasant room. In the darkness he walked from the station, and in the room made tea, there was almost no milk, some soured in a bottle in the flywire safe. At the table he worked without haste, it was almost light when he took off his clothes, lay on the bed, seeing the thin branches take shape against the curtain. The next two mornings he worked, and for a time at night, in the afternoons walking the streets among the suburban houses, the gardens. On the second afternoon as far as the river, walking fast, effort in itself. When he came back he read the pages, and it was there. Existing. The men. And the girl. The smooth glowing trunks of the salmon gums. There was the form, the words in their fall, their place. But they are not now, he said. Not of this time. Of these streets. A childhood and a past. To be exorcised perhaps. Yet an image.

The rain drove across the balcony, streaked the long glass doors. The heavy leaves of a creeper swung at the glass.

A day to bring your car, Maria said.

It will pass over. He picked up one of the minute sweet biscuits she served with coffee. Though she would not call them biscuits. A secret, she said. I left the car, he said. I wanted to take the train.

A disturbing thought.

A psychodelic journey. Time travel.

Yes, she said. But was it necessary?

I think so. For what I've been trying to do.

I mean, it is everywhere. Bus shelters. Subways. Any stray piece of fencing. Everywhere.

Yes.

Doesn't it disturb you?

I've seen it before, he said. When I suppose you could say it was less obtrusive. Less assertive perhaps. But yes. It does.

She set her cup down. James wants you to do this chapter. And he is sorry he had to go to Brisbane.

He didn't tell me.

He didn't want to postpone this.

Well I'm glad, he said.
And you will do the chapter?
I don't mean about the chapter.
No. I was afraid you didn't. Why don't you want to do it?
I've told you, Maria.
This is a caring book.
A strange word.
Strange?
I don't remember it at all once.
I don't remember a lot of things once.
James wouldn't take what I would have to write about forests. Forest use. Forest reserves. Our quaint concept that we can eradicate them and still have them. The little boy who eats the cake and says he still has it.
But the book will offer a view of all this.
I'm sick of all the hypocrisy.
You don't have to be hypocritical. God, what a word. Just be your usual bastard self.
I'll send him the chapter. He can send it back.
I hoped you'd see reason.
Reason, Maria, is not what you're about.
No. It isn't, is it.
I'm glad of that anyhow. And of your coffee.
And will you make a psychodelic return? Or shall I drive you.
I've made my journey, he said. Yes please.
She watched the rain against the glass. Sitting quite still. Her dark hair, the dark dress. With all the rain, she said, at least there's no hurry. It is not a day for trains.

KILL   **PIGS**

      a land of flowers

deth to the   Karen

                                                                    ooooooooo

                  chas!

                       BAN URANIUM SALES

                          fucks
             Wimmin for Peace

                                                     FRED

OUT   SHITTT

                                                                FUCK
                                                                   E
                                                                   N

                 WAR

       aaaaaaah!

                                             ANARCHY

There were cracks in the pavement, a long line he had not noticed, thin flat leaves pushing at the grey surface. The light clear, but with the sense of haze. Later the street would be without shade. A woman pushed a broom at the boards of a verandah, two doors down on the other side. Aware of him. The sweepings falling to the small space between the verandah and the fence. He heard the lock move slowly on the door, and she said: You.

He said: It doesn't matter if it's not a good time.

You're a stranger.

She wore a black robe, a purple thread woven to an intricate pattern across the shoulders and back. In the room she yawned. Lifted her arm. The robe sliding on her thin white shoulders. Early, she said. I'll make coffee. Or if you want a drink.

Too early for that, he said. I'm sorry, but I thought I'd probably miss you if I came later.

I'm here most of the time.

There was the same furniture. Placed the same. Nothing on the mantel. As she came in with coffee, holding easily the two cups, she said: I put them away. Most things. Bits and pieces worry me.

Are you all right?

Good.

Your two men?

No. Not any more. A while back one of them came and said they'd got no deal with Harry now. They thought he'd gone to Queensland. I sat and listened.

And that was it?

Nothing more. Just a kind of look around. They'd got whatever time they wanted to fix things. I was like Harry now. Dead.

The bastards. But it would be like that.

The place is full of bastards. It's like you just try to get by with one that's a bit less.

Harry always called you an optimist.

Is it okay with you?

Problems. Your man didn't give you the coffee when he left?

She slid the black robe across her leg. Her nails probing. There are still things in this house that bite. No. He was giving nothing. Other men. I've got a couple of Americans. Nice guys. One wants me to go back to the States with him. After.

That.

He could probably work it.

Would you?

It's just bullshit with this guy. But for real, I might.

Don't.

They're moving out anyhow. They reckon it's nearly over. I might have to move. I'm not going to be wanted round here. That worries me.

Go back west?

Not unless I have to. You?

Not to Perth. And if I went back to the land it would swallow me. That scares me. I don't think I can ever get away from that.

You're a funny bugger. There'll be money around after.

For a while. At least there won't be checking up all the time. Where you go. What you do. When you shit.

I wouldn't bet on that, Rene.

She crossed her legs, leaned back in the chair, the robe a dark line along her thigh. She said: Are things bad?

Nothing definite. I just get the feeling they've found out about me being close to Harry. Nerves, maybe.

They've buried that. It was nothing to them.

There was the money. It's like losing my nerve, I think. I've got problems that will come up later, as well as what's going on now.

You and all the rest.

True. But in the middle of the night I wake up running. I've been thinking about Sydney. It's supposed to be not so organised up there. Not as tight as here.

If it's money.

It is money. As well.

If you're serious, she said, Harry gave me an address in Sydney. If I needed it. The way it's worked out it's not going to be that. But if it's any help. You'd have to watch the trains.

I wouldn't go by train. I could get a ride up, offsiding on a truck. They go up the back way and it can be a bit rough. But if there's anyone looking for me, that could be off. If they know.

I don't think there's anyone. It wouldn't be that hard if they wanted to. It's always like that. It was like that with Harry. I don't know how much he ever knew. How much anyone knew. When it's over I just might go back west. There are times this gives me the shits. Do you want the address?

Please.

Why don't we just put in the day drinking?

Here?

Or down the Castle. Well, the morning anyway. I've got one of my Americans coming this afternoon. She stood up suddenly, stepped across to the window. She did not move the thin curtain. The shadow had drawn back from the street. This bloody place, she said.

The shadows in the room had moved. The front window curtains drawn, the floor had been dark, the walls distant. Now from the side a line of light crossed the bed, angled towards the table, across the papers and books. The curtain of the side window drifted slightly. He closed his eyes. The sound at the door tentative. He did not move in the bed. He could reach the small window. Roll to the ground. Under the house. Lie with the rubbish of years. No more than the movement of the light. The shadow. The fall. Without sound. The movie star balancing on a fourteenth storey window. The moment of safety as the car flashed in front of the express. Perhaps they had known it all. Left nothing. She said: Please. It's me. Jessica.

As she had been in the film. The frames flickering. The white made-up face turning to the camera. Listening at the unopened door. She said: What is it? Please.

Nothing much, he said. She moved past him into the room. A film, I think.

A film?

An old silent. I think we were both in it.

She stood near the door, as if she had not entered the room, her hands at her sides, the handbag held against her. She had a tightfitting hat that emphasised her face, drawing her hair back, held to her neck. She said: You look very ill. You should be in bed.

I was.

Have you been trying to write a film script? Is that what you mean?

No. Just the light.

You said something about us being like in a film before. Why do you say that?

Because I think we are. And you are cinematic.

If you are ill you need to be somewhere you can be looked after. Not in this place.

No hospitals. Doctors. I don't need that.

I think obviously you do.

It's just an attack. If I'm careful it will pass. I've had it before.

I could take you to a doctor.

I can't go to doctors and I can't go to hospitals. Just leave me to get over it.

No, she said. Lie down while I try to work something out. Have you been eating?

I can't eat. I have to drink a lot of water. Fruit juice.

She put her bag on the table. Her hands lifted quickly to her hat. Releasing it. She said: What is funny?

Nothing, he said. Your hat. It's part of all this mad thing. They had hats like that in the old silent movies.

No doubt. I'll make you a drink. Is there anything in your kitchen?

I haven't been out.

What are you supposed to have?

Orange. Lemons are best. You won't like the kitchen. God you're like an army. You should go, Jessica. I can manage.

He lay on the bed and he felt cold. He pulled the blanket over himself, but it was nothing to do with the covering. The nausea rose strongly, and he might simply have leaned out the window. Above the midden. Except it was not that kind of nausea and he knew he was afraid.

She walked quietly. Unlike the woman in the house. Who must have been out or there would have been the noise of the child. He did not hear her in the passage. She closed the door.

The place is hopeless. It's no wonder you're ill.

I might always have this. It's things I eat. And drink. And worry, I think.

You can't be here like this.

I can't not be here. You don't understand.

I understand enough. Do you think I could stay here until you're well enough?

You can't stand the place.

There's only one thing, she said. If you won't go to hospital. You can come to my place.

I wish you'd just go.

I couldn't do that. At least there you can rest and have some kind of care.

And your friends?

They needn't know. And if they do, well, it's not going to matter.

All this bloody thing, he said, this war, is nearly over. Or that's what they say. I might just see it out. You'll have to go, Jessica. I can't come to your place. This thing is supposed to be infectious. What happens if we both go down with it?

We'll have to share the bed, I suppose.

Your sense of humour is a bit off. And a bit late, maybe.

I'll get a taxi, she said. And throw out that rubbish in that kitchen of yours. They might condemn it before you come back if I left it.

They don't condemn things out here. Leave it for the mice.

The day had no distinction, its passing the fall of light, the pattern of shadow, the single window, curtained. The sounds from the street, from the building, voices, shadow and sound fused to the sense of people at the door and they were taking her away. Into silence. Voices mechanical, words distinguishing themselves and yet the same, a kind of precision, the couple who lived in the other part of the house, deaf, she had said, their bulletins, timed exact. The thick tree above the window and the mulberries he had picked for her. He wanted to tell her. The thin curtains of the window shaded the room and he was glad of the shadow. Of her coming in the middle of the day. She made him fruit drinks, he saw the jug on the table, the rows of fruit in the shops, the barrows on the streets, layers of colour, surprising him when he had first come here. She cooked light food, made him jellies, red, yellow, one a deep rich purple, steady in their dishes, sculpted. Very good, he said. We had those when I was a child. I had forgotten them. I have asked about this, she said. And what you can eat. You shouldn't say anything, he said. I can't be here. In the evening she sat in the bedroom, worked about the flat. She did not play any of the records, but asked if he would like her to read to him. I don't have anything you'd like. Nothing at all, really. I could read to you about fashions. But some of your books. The ones you brought. I'd forgotten, he said. Forgotten I did bring any. She said: You did. And some of your papers. In that small case. You said you couldn't leave them. Do you remember what else you said? Probably I do. Or near enough. But you should forget. I was a bit confused at the time. Yes you were. And you said the bastards will read them. They could use them. Your papers I think you meant. I remember, he said. I remember you giving the case to the taxi driver. Did you understand what I was saying? I don't want to, she said. It doesn't matter. Shall I read to you? Some of them are political, he said. Hopes for a future. And hopes for saving something of the country itself. The land. Water. Soil. I don't think they'd read too well. This one, if you like. Grossman. *The People Immortal*. Propagandist, but I haven't read anything like it before, almost no modern Russian writing. I found it in a bookshop in Bourke Street. I was thinking about it and some of the painting here. Do you think they are, she said. Immortal? I doubt it. He moved towards sleep to her quiet voice that held little emphasis, careful, even. A cadence. It was dark when she had gone. Sleeping in the other room, on the lounge. It's stupid, he said. You can't do that. She laughed. You're infectious. Not changing in the bedroom, taking her clothes from the long wardrobes, racks of dresses. She left him the day's paper, the headlines, the careful statements, it will soon be over, she said. No, he said. Not while they can find people to kill. And not here, while there are generals to occupy fooling about with endless islands. She said: You are very bitter, but she would not argue.

Late one afternoon, when he had been asleep, she came into the room with a small paper covered book, black, red lettering. He saw it clearly in her hands. She said: Can I read you something? A poem. I was looking at this while you were asleep. *Phoenix*, he said. The Adelaide University. Some very brilliant people. I picked it up in a sixpenny box. A measure of our regard. She read slowly, letting the lines fall, at times not sure of their pattern.

> This wound will hold some truth perhaps
> In time future, when the knife is lost,
> And the hand which held it clasps
> Elsewhere a sheet in death.
>
> For you the afternoon may be enough,
> And in the evening the shadow of the moth;
> You may not see the mind rebuff
> The shadow on the floor.
>
> But the fool who laughs will hear
> Dead steps in the hollow hills,
> And as again they echo near
> This wound will hold some truth perhaps.

It's haunting, she said. I think I feel like you did about the quartet. But I don't think I understand it. I feel it somehow.

Feeling is enough, he said. Though I doubt we could say that to the poets in that magazine. Donald Kerr was a very fine poet.

Was?

He was killed in the war.

Then it is just too sad, she said. She put the book down and went suddenly from the room.

Later, in the evening, she played some recordings, tentative, uncertain, as if he might object. She said: I told you about the *Triple Concerto*. I was able to get it. Would you like to hear it?

If it's not like that quartet. I don't think I'm well enough to survive that.

She looked at the record in her hands. The clear blue label. This is different.

She was quiet, unobtrusive in turning the records, aware of him. As if she wanted him to like the music. It is different, he said. Another world. The patterns of sound that had risen, and clashed, drawn one another, agreed. Yes. When she came home next evening he said: I've been thinking about your concerto. I'd like to write a novel like that. Does that make sense?

I think so. Yes, she said. Yes it does.

Except it would most likely come out like the quartet. Those great surges are not for me. That soaring assertion. Not for anyone any longer. How could they be. The waste land.

She touched his hand quickly. I'm sorry. If that's true. And I suppose it is.

She did not want his help, with the flat, the kitchen, this in some way personal to her. He took the couch to sleep, and she went back to the bedroom. It's like the walls of Jericho, he said. That film. Clark Gable.

Yes, she said. It is in a way. You don't mind?

She was standing close to him, looking at him with an odd seriousness. How should I mind. You've done a kind of miracle. For me. Can I ask you a question?

I don't think I want you to. But if you like.

When I was going to come and listen to your recording,

the concerto, and you had a visitor for the week. Did you have a good week?

Not exactly a visitor for the week. The way you put it. He didn't stay here. No, I didn't. It was my fault.

We could walk, he said. Around a few of your streets.

The streets quiet, darkened, they walked slowly. In the sidestreets hedges and shrubs edging the pavements. She said: We had better not go too far.

I can walk, he said. I'm fine now. Thanks to you. I can leave you in peace.

What will you do?

Go back to my fine big room.

And there?

Go on with what I've been doing. It doesn't have to make sense to anyone else. I can't be concerned with anyone looking in. However they see it.

I didn't mean that.

What I'm involved in is a sort of survival exercise. And I've no idea how long it has to go on.

After the war, after all this, will it be the same?

I'll have to find some kind of work. I want to study. Something like postgraduate work. It would have to be Australian history, if I can find somewhere it exists. That would be at least some lead into Australian writing. There's nowhere I could study that.

Surely there must be.

No. In the face of all that's been happening in our own country, no.

We should go back, she said. If we go round here it leads back to the house. Do you think we could have a holiday?

I've been having one. At your expense.

That's so stupid. No, go away somewhere. It doesn't have to be for long. We have a cottage at Apollo Bay. My family. The cousins. All of us. It's always empty now.

What about your job?

I haven't had a holiday for ages.

I thought you had a week off just a while ago.

No. I didn't. That was part of what was wrong. I don't want to think about that. Could we go there?

Just when I think I've worked out some things about you, he said, I find I haven't. We could, if you say so.

You'd be the only one thinks there's anything to work out. I'm glad we can go.

In the morning he said: Jessica, it's not possible.

She was dressed. Ready to leave for the day. She said: I knew you wouldn't go.

Don't look like that. I don't think you understand.

You always say that.

The plain bloody fact is I haven't the money.

She stepped towards him quickly, her hand touching his arm. That's nothing. The cottage won't cost anything. I told you no one uses it.

All the rest will cost something.

I don't care about money. I'll lend it to you. You can pay me back.

If you don't care about money it's because you have it.

That's not true. And it's a cruel thing to say.

I'm not trying to be cruel. I'm not trying to be anything.

I know that, she said. And I have to go. It's my turn to open the shop this week. I'll see you tonight.

Yes.

You will be here?

Yes, he said.

The casually placed MPs. Others not in any uniform that marked them. Lines of people by the carriages. She brushed against him, swung by the moving crowd.

Why are you so serious?

I was looking at you.

The cream coloured blouse, jacket with sleeves to her elbows. Her arms faintly brown, hardly a colour at all. Her smooth hair. She said: I don't mind that.

She held close to him, as if he might have turned at the last step and walked away down the platform.

It's still like a film, he said. Will they or won't they get on the train.

We are on it. But yes, it is like that. Like you might suddenly not be here. Or I'm lost in all these people.

There was the flat country, the same as the day he first came to the city. When it had been raining. A greyness, and cold. From Geelong the motor coach and the curves of road cut from the cliff face, the drop to rocks and sea. Long lines of waves. A long way down, he said. If you meet someone coming too fast.

Not many cars this far out, she said. Not with the rationing.

Quite a few are putting their hopes on that.

What do you mean?

Those little bits of paper will be gold. I'm not sure this road was meant for cars. For your friend Joyce, perhaps. One of her horses.

Then the road ran level, close to the sea, and there was the beach and the small town, pine trees dark along the waterfront. Behind it the hills, bare and folded, the high dead trees against the sky.

Stunted ti tree, rounded by the wind, screened the cottage. Smaller trees along one side had been burned, showed a sharp green undergrowth. I don't know who did that, she said. Under a water tank at the back pot plants were set out, all but two dead, the soil dry. She moved some of the pots. The key, she said. It should be here.

The cottage smaller, simpler, than he expected, they did not come here often, she had said. Something they had perhaps grown out of. Yet attractive. Three rooms, the back door opening to a wide room the length of the cottage, two front rooms, their doors open, used as bed rooms. In the main room a wood stove, a long table, wooden chairs. There were cupboards, a dresser with china that held the faint light. She drew back the curtains and across the gap in the ti tree he could see the dark pines of the settlement, the line of hills holding the bay. They walked in to the town for food, coming back along the path by the long jetty, the fishing boats further out, one against the jetty. You can buy fish from them, she said. He brought in wood for the stove, the bay darkening, heavy shadow lengthening from the hills. The lamp in the room gave a soft light, without glare. He set a fire in the stove, cleaning the top and the hearth.

This stove will test your cooking. It's like a smaller version of the one we had at home. My mother was a good cook. There were a few hard years there, but I never remember us being hungry.

There was a big kitchen in the old house, she said. And a huge stove. Far too big. It was built for when there were servants.

We never had many houses like that over there. None like the bigger houses here. I never realised how small it all was until I came here.

It's very big on the map.

All bluff. It's strange how you like your old house.

Not strange at all. A house like that can be more real than people.

One day I might drive past and peer over the fence.

You wouldn't see it. It's all hidden from the road.

In the front room, to the left of the kitchen, she said I always have this room, she opened the suitcase they had brought, taking out her clothes, a pair of sheets. Blankets and a rug folded in one of the cupboards, she spread the sheets quickly, easily. Do your side, she said.

Are the walls coming down?

You don't have to laugh at me.

I like to laugh at you. The bed's very fine. If I get in there I'm not sure I'll want to get out.

Perhaps you won't have to. She said: I want to go outside and I'm afraid of that horrible loo out there. When I was a child and we were here I hated going out there at night. I used to say I didn't need to, but that wasn't always such a good idea.

You can take the lamp.

That makes it worse. Creepy shadows. Leave the door open.

He watched the shadows move across the path, the dark frame of the tankstand shifting, forming, the flame flatten in the wind. In the room she undressed without haste, hanging her clothes in the big cupboard that was half wardrobe. As if unaware of him. Perhaps, a part of her work, being seen, looked at. In that other world, a model. Displaying her own designs. Fabrics. He said: I've never seen you like that.

I'm frightened.

You can't be.

Yes.

I was thinking you were so, I don't know, remote. As if I wasn't here.

It's not of anything you'd understand. But this place. It's so cut off. Alone, I mean.

And you're caught here with someone you don't know.

I do know you. Of course it's not that.

I don't know what you mean, he said. But if you somehow think I expect this, that you have to do something you don't want to, then it's just not like that. No, I don't know what you mean.

He touched her shoulders, white, her skin untouched by the sun, her body slender, small breasts. Her thighs long, rounded. His fingers traced lightly along her shoulders. You should model your dresses. The things in your shop.

Do you do that?

Sometimes. I'm not a model. They come from the agency.

You could be.

I might.

Perhaps you were right about this place. We stand here like this talking about your shop.

Yes. Though that's not what I meant.

The light was filtered by the curtain, absorbed and changed by the old furniture of the room, the cupboard, brown smooth wood, the walls themselves, a glow.

It's early, she said.

Almost eight. If that's early.

The light on her body, there too absorbed, changed, her shoulders, her back. You're a kind of gold, he said. Light. Like one of those small golden flowers that blow away in the wind when you touch them. I'm sorry if that's early morning poetic.

Am I like that?

Now. Yes.

I'm not very used to this, am I.

What does that mean?

You know very well.

Does that somehow matter?

I was afraid it would.

I'm not sure I know you at all.

Sometimes I think I'm just afraid. Of all sorts of things. There was only Charles. And it was rather horrible. I don't want to say that. I shouldn't. It was what I meant last night. I was just suddenly alone here and it could all have been impossible.

You don't need to talk about it.

But I do. I've never been able to talk about anything. Least this. My parents, I think they felt if I'd been watching the animals on the farm there was nothing they needed to say. I've tried to talk to Joyce, but she only laughs. She was very knowing when we were young. Nothing like that seemed to bother her. She just accepted, I suppose. I did wonder if she really knew any more than I did.

It is the big silence. It was for our generation. For this country. You still can't write about it. A matter of luck, more or less.

Yes. Like you are for me.

No, he said. Please. You shouldn't say things like that.

Why?

Thomas Hardy. The fates listen.

Is he one of your friends?

He held her suddenly. You should be serious about the great.

We could walk along the beach. Take our lunch. It's such a lovely day.

You do frighten me, he said.

Where the road ended they walked along a narrow track through the dunes, a thin scrub holding the sand. Wide flat rock shelves stretched to a point, the land higher behind them, the rock grey and smooth, broken at its outer edges to points and clefts. Red anemones were closed to limp bulbs in the shallow pools. Open, their arms clear, where the water deepened. Small starfish, a few alone, clutched the sand, under the ledges of rock in colonies, still, waiting for the returning water, shellfish holding the rocks against the suck of the waves.

I'd forgotten there were things like this here, she said. Or perhaps they were not here then.

They probably were. There might be more now because the holiday makers don't come. Benefits of war.

You think the war has helped them.

I think it has, yes. We can kill ourselves now. Not other things. It makes a change.

I won't think like that, she said. There's something in you scares me. I won't think about it.

Are you cold?

Not in this sun. Wonderful.

Around the point the mouth of a creek cut a thin opening over the sand. The body of a penguin moved with the waves, tangled in the thick brown kelp. Two more at the edge of the water. There is another in the weed, she said. Why are they like this.

Caught in the fishing nets, possibly.

She lifted one of the heavy strands of kelp, still slick and wet. It's like harness. We should take some for Joyce. She came here with us one school holiday. But it rained a lot. I didn't like it.

The long brown strip slid from her hand. I can't touch the penguins. But we shouldn't leave them there.

The sea will take them.

I know.

Walk, he said. Come on.

They lay on the sand, sheltered from the wind by the rock ledges, she rested her head on his arm and she was soon asleep. As they walked back, across the bay the hills were shrouded with haze that held smoke from the country behind them. They seemed distant, shadowed, the colour dulled.

In the morning he brought in wood for the fire and she insisted she should cook breakfast. You wouldn't care, she said. You've starved yourself. Someone has to look after you.

Later they walked to the shops where she went in to buy the things she said they needed. White clouds moved above the hills, the shadows across the slopes. Clouds oddly shaped, like reflections of the hills themselves. He took the parcels from her. She was holding a folded newspaper. He said: The world.

I suppose it doesn't make much sense here.

Not much. None.

But you read the papers. I left them for you when you were ill.

Pieces of them. One day someone is going to write a history of the organised lies we've been told over the last ten years.

And would that person be you?

Not me. I've believed too many of them.

She let the paper fall into an open drum by the path, cut as a rubbish container. It's gone, she said. She held his arm and they walked slowly. In the cottage she put the things away, tidied the table and shelves.

We could go down to the beach, he said. If we started soon. When you're finished. Say before dark.

I'll get some lunch.

We've just had breakfast.

You should eat.

It's a wonder you keep that body of yours the way it is.

I eat properly, she said. And there's nothing wrong with liking to cook.

The wind was cold, they walked along the road to cut across to the beach further down than they had been the day before, by an old quarry in the grey eroded rocks.

There must be fossils in these mudstones, he said. All this once a great sea of life.

There were the flat worn pavements at the broken stretches of beach. The grey scrub covered dunes rose behind the beach and the rocks. In a curve of beach cut between two arms of grey rock that changed to deeper colour as the waves washed over it a small surf broke. He took off his clothes and ran at the breaking waves. It's too cold, she said. And I don't like swimming. When he lay in the warmth, face down on the dry sand by the rock wall, she trickled a fine pattern of sand over his back. She said: You don't know what I've written.

No, he said.

When he turned on his side, she watched the sand slide slowly across his skin, ridges of it still holding.

Brush it off, he said.

She moved her hand, then stopped. No.

The stove warmed the room, she cleared the table and they washed the things she had used for the meal. They could wait till the morning, he said.

I don't like to start the day like that.

No worse than finishing it like this.

Much worse.

They pushed the chairs before the stove and he built the fire. The room was quiet, the faint sound of the metal of the stove heating.

It's very quiet. I'd be afraid here by myself.

I never minded the night, he said. Or silence. Part of the way I grew up.

Would you like to stay here?

This could be a good place to complete a piece of work. But not to stay.

You could use it if you wanted to. For as long as you liked.

Your family might have something to say about that.

I don't think they would mind at all.

I might have to go to Sydney.

She spread her hands slowly, her fingers held against the narrow slit in the doors of the stove, the orange glow of the wood behind them.

You can't do that.

It may be I can't not do it.

You won't tell me.

We might not have to worry about it, he said. Not for a time.

The war is going to be over. It will be ended.

Yes. If you look at it that way.

A light rain smeared the windows, cutting across dust he had not noticed, grey over the tops of the ti trees. She was asleep, and he lay beside her, her face turned on the pillow, her hair held, as if she had arranged it, across the side of her face. He touched it with his lips and she did not move. Outside the greyness faded in the gaining light.

It was late when she woke, and he had slept again. He said: The day has gone.

She lifted herself slowly. No. But it's been raining. You didn't tell me.

You weren't here.

We could take our lunch and walk up into the hills. Could we do that? The Wild Dog Road?

It's too late. Tomorrow.

Tomorrow then. I'll make a good lunch. We could buy one of those fish from the boats later. For dinner.

It's an obsession.

She lay beside him and he said: I didn't know it was going to be like this.

You must have.

Why should I?

Well yes. Why should you.

Will it be all right?

I think so. She watched the pattern on the window, the squares of glass that themselves made a pattern she had not seen before. Suppose it was not?

I'm not in much of a position to do anything about it. I'm sorry, he said. But that's the plain fact.

Never mind. It never has. I'm sure we'll be lucky.

Two boats were moored to the jetty. On one the men gutted fish, their actions smooth, precise, throwing the fish cleanly onto the jetty. The pieces drifted down in the clear water and near a patch of weed the flat bulk of a ray moved about the bits. They bought a fish, it must be four feet long, she said. You carry it. He cleaned it by the tank outside the cottage.

The road climbed steeply, turning near the creek they had seen at the beach, curving with the folds and spurs of the hills. To the right, as they walked, the ground rose steeply above them, on the other side, at the edge of the road, dropped to the narrow watercourse at the bottom of the deep gully. The hills above the gully cleared and bare of timber. A boundary fence cut a straight line upward, bracken green and thick over the slope of the hill, the dark shapes of regrown trees. On the other side of the fence the hill cleared, a few dead trees white on the high slopes, sharp eroded paths like terraces. There were cattle in the bed of the gully.

She said: How did they ever get down there.

How did they ever herd animals over those hills. A better question would by why.

Perhaps they didn't.

Perhaps they didn't. Whoever was on this side of the fence got tired of it. And somebody cleared all this. Whatever happened to it later. It's a strange destruction.

A bit sad.

More than a bit. Yes.

Further into the hills the timber was thicker and the sun came through the haze among the high trees along the ridges. Cloud moved low over the rounded hills and rain came across the slopes, grey, along the gully. The rain washed over them, hitting them as it had the trunks of the trees above the road. The shower passed and the heat brought a sudden steam from the road, the dead grass on the near slopes sodden and flat. The rain moved away down the valley and across the hills.

It's like that fence line, she said. You could run along behind it and be quite dry.

On the high bank above the road she unwrapped the

lunch she had prepared, the sun drying them. The bracken in the paddocks was a deep green.

It's a strange place, she said. Could you write about it?

It's an odd question. But no. I don't think so. I should think some painters might get something out of the bones and skeletons of those hills.

No one could live here. I think it frightens me.

They have tried, he said. It may have frightened them.

But it has a kind of beauty. I think I'd never really seen these hills.

As they came back onto the road by the bay, the hills behind them, the rain came sharply, running out of their clothes, out of their hair, and she turned to him laughing. Who needs clothes, she said. It's the wild dog, he said. You disturbed him. The water slopped in their shoes. In the cottage he made the fire, she brought towels and they stripped their clothes and stood before the stove. Her skin took colour from the heat. She stared at the glow of the burning wood, still, as though she had forgotten the cold, though her skin held a faint roughness. He held the towel about her shoulders, moved it slowly down her back. Those strange hills, she said. They were so beautiful.